GRIFFIN BROTHERS BOOK 5

KATHI S. BARTON

This is a work of fiction. Names, characters, places, and incidents are products of the author's imagination or are used fictitiously and are not to be construed as real. Any resemblance to actual events, locations, organizations, or persons, living or dead, is entirely coincidental.

World Castle Publishing, LLC
Pensacola, Florida
Copyright © 2024 Kathi S. Barton
Hardback ISBN: 9798891262096
Paperback ISBN: 9798891262102
eBook ISBN: 9798891262119
First Edition World Castle Publishing, LLC, May 3, 2024
http://www.worldcastlepublishing.com
Licensing Notes
All rights reserved. No part of this book may be used or reproduced in any manner whatsoever without written permission, except in the case of brief quotations embodied in articles and reviews.
Cover: Karen Fuller
Editor: Karen Fuller

Prologue

Charles, Charlie to most people who knew him, was so lost that he hadn't any idea if he was walking on the ground or the sky. He knew the difference, of course, but it was so dark out tonight that if there had been a moon shining, he couldn't see it. When he sat himself down on a log to get his bearings again, he paused in his thinking to look at what could have made the sound he'd heard.

Terrified out of his mind when he saw glowing eyes looking at him, Charlie sat as still as he could. The eyes grew larger and incredibly more shiny as the beast made his way to him. He didn't run, knowing that even if he knew where he was at the moment, the wolf would know it better. It would chase him down and kill him without any hesitation.

The wolf, a big gray fella, just stood there within

a few inches of his outstretched legs. When he laid down, putting his heavy head onto his leg, Charlie had another moment of fear. The thing never took his eyes off him either. As soon as he felt he was brave enough to try and talk to the wolf, he was gone, and a man was in his place.

A fully clothed man with the gray of the wolf's fur colored into his hair. Even his eyes were the same as the wolf, Charlie thought. Still, neither of them moved until the man sat back on his butt and regarded him.

"You live on the property not far from here, is that correct?" Charlie told him he was only squatting there until they found him. But he was a mite lost. "Yes, I've been following you for some time. And in all that time, you didn't harm any other animal you came across, and there were plenty of them, too. Why is that?"

"You mean the rabbit and the family of deer?" The man nodded. "I don't have a need for meat just now. I only kill when I have to. When my belly feels like it can't go another minute without some meat in it. And even then, I use it up to the best I can. What I can't use, I find some other animal that will use the rest. Why do you ask?"

"I'll get to that. You didn't seem that surprised

when I changed from wolf to man. Can you tell me why that is?" He nodded and told him what he'd been seeing a lot of lately. "Yes, war will make a man wish for better times. So you were surprised, but you just wrote it off as being another strange thing that had no explanation. That's a very good reason, I think."

"They say that the war is about over. I don't know much about that. I can still hear shooting when I'm out and about. I don't have any land left because the soldiers took it all when they was coming through. Not that it was much more than a bunch of rocks and stumps to begin with." The man only nodded. "I'm Charles Griffin. Most call me Charlie. A great deal more, but I ignore them. Not everybody was able to go to school all the time. I had my family to feed when my daddy up and got sick. Momma died a few weeks ago, and I've been roaming around since looking for work. I don't suppose you know anyone that might be wanting an extra hand around or two, do you?"

"I do, as a matter of fact. My name is Romeo Hank. The Hank is for when I need a last name. But I do have something that I'd like to propose to you if you've got the time to listen." Charlie told him he didn't have anything but time right now. "All right. "I have a medium-sized pack. You can see a few of them over there watching over us. They're all just wolves. I'm the only wolf shifter that I know. They're a good bunch. Hungry most of the time, but then all of us are, correct?"

"Yes. Some more than others. At least I can find me a bit of string and fashion me up a hook to use." Romeo told him that was excellent. "You need me to fish some fish out for you and your pack? I don't mind at all doing that for you. In fact, I'd be powerful happy to help you out."

"Not just yet. But I think that I will take you up on it soon. I have a daughter. Her name is Luna. Such a beautiful name, don't you think?" Charlie asked if it meant moon. "It does. Thank you. You're very well educated for a man with no means of living."

"My mom was a school teacher when I was born. They fired her, of course, when she had me. She didn't know my daddy, so that didn't help her none. She taught me to read and to figure. I can write too but I do have to think about the spelling of things. Can you write?" Romeo said that he'd been given a great gift in that. "I think so too. When I find me a newspaper or some little old book, I treasure it for a bit. Then, I pass it on if I can. I don't have to know the people in the paper. I just like reading about their stories. Are you going to tell me what this is about?"

"I am. I was working up to it but I believe you to be a man that can be trusted with things in life. I would like to change you into a wolf. One such as I am. You'll be a man when you wish. A wolf when necessary. There will be magic as well as wealth." Charlie told him he didn't have use for wealth, but food all the time would be nice. "That is precisely what I'm speaking about, Charlie, my good man."

Throughout the rest of the night and well into the morning, they spoke of things that Romeo needed from him. It wasn't brought up again about him being changed, but Romeo did tell him that his daughter and found out that he, plain old Charlie was her mate. The soul reason that he'd not been harmed while wandering around in the woods.

"Do you understand what it is I want you to do?" Charlie said that he thought so. "No. I'm sorry. I can't allow you to go into this only thinking you understand. Please, ask me anything that you'd like. You must be clear on this. I need for you to be clear on how it is. I wish for you to someday take over for me."

Romeo never got upset with him when he asked his questions. If Charlie was honest with himself, which he usually tried not to be, he was afraid that Romeo had picked the wrong man. That he'd be better off finding himself someone else to take over his empire.

"You're the right man, Charlie. When I told you that I'd been following you around, I wanted you to know that it wasn't just last evening. But for some time now. I've seen you share your last bit of food with people. Work for someone who cannot do for themselves and not take anything but a bit of bread and water. You're a very good man. A better man that I am." Charlie started to protest. "No. I'm correct in picking you as my replacement. And if that is some of your worry, being an Alpha, you've no worries there either. I will not leave this earth for the next until you are comfortable with what is needed of you. Now. If you've no more questions, I shall leave you to allow you to think on it. I'll be back here tomorrow so that you can tell me your answer. I know I have picked the right man, Charlie. It's something that you can do easily to save this pack and my daughter."

Luna followed him as he walked around. He'd thought about calling Romeo back and asking more questions, but he didn't. Sitting down again, his leg bothering him from sitting so long, he looked at the big, beautiful wolf.

"You're not really his daughter, are you?" She

shook her head. "I didn't think so. Is there any more of the others that he claims are his children?" She nodded this time, and he determined by asking questions that it was one other female. "I don't know what to think about all this, to be honest with you. Are you my mate? Is he telling me the truth? I just don't know what to think."

She nodded or shook her head after each of the questions he put to her. Yes, she was his mate. Yes, Romeo was telling the truth. There were many more questions and answers. He was headed back to the area where he'd first seen Romeo when he felt the pain take his breath away as it slammed into his left shoulder.

Falling back, he hit his head and laid there while trying his best to catch his breath. That was when he heard the other gun shots, the wolf howling and trying to hide. Pulling Luna toward him, he whispered harshly into her ear, hoping that at least she'd understand him enough to know that she must warn the others.

"Go. Tell Romeo to hide the pack. To make sure you and your sister are safe." She didn't want to leave him, whimpering at him as she laid her head on his shoulder. "Go. Please. Run and escape before they hurt you, too."

When she left him, Charlie closed his eyes.

Opening them when he felt the shadow darken over him, he looked up in time to see the barrel of a large rifle. He was a goner. He knew that. He could only hope that Luna and the others were safe.

Chapter 1

Harman was glad that he'd been able to leave the hospital, but he wasn't as sure that he was fit enough to be living on his own like the doctor had told him and was glad now that he'd gone to stay with his parents for the first few days. Being pampered was the best when his mom did it.

Twice now, he'd fallen over when reaching for something just beyond his reach and overestimated his ability to get something. So, he needed to call the doctor again before he did something permanent to his noggin. His mom came in the back door, and he nearly sobbed, he was so happy to see her. She'd been out pulling the last of the garden things out of her plot out back.

A week ago, he'd been volunteering at the hospital, feeding babies, changing diapers, and such.

He'd really enjoyed it, all of it that had anything to do with his plan of playing nursemaid to the little ones. Not to mention, he also had learned a great deal about babies too. Since his brothers were finding their mates, and some children were coming along, he thought of himself as an expert on changing the diaper in record time. But he had also hated the job.

Harman had been planning to write a book that he knew would be fun to write. He was still going to write one but things had evolved into something more when he was working with the nurses. He'd never met a more bitter group of women than he had in the nursery department. He was sure that it was only this department at this hospital as he'd not run into it at other places he'd been.

It had started out with it being a book, a manual, so to speak, about what babies and mothers, too, had to go through before they were able to take their little ones home. He was also going to suggest things that the nurses and staff told him that would be helpful to new parents as to what they will need as opposed to what they might not. However, working with three or four nurses who were caring for the babies had gossiped every day about what the children would have to endure—in their opinion—when they got home. They made every parent sound like they were drug addicts as well as mooching off the government's tit — in their opinion. He'd heard that several times and 'popping' out babies so they'd get more money. They didn't know half of what they were talking about, he soon discovered and had been, but not taken seriously, asking them not to talk about others in his presence.

So he'd taken notes on what their lives were up to so as to show them that they were no better. The things that they did while working to compensate themselves for being 'short-changed' for being a nurse. A job that they specifically went to college for. Stealing was the biggest factor in these ladies' lives right after badmouthing people who weren't at their best when bringing a new life into the world.

When he was leaving after telling them off, one of them picked up a fire extinguisher and knocked him on his ass. Before going down, he was hit again and then a third time. Had he been human, he would have died then, but he did end up in the hospital for several days with a concussion as well as a hundred stitches in his head alone. He'd found out later that they had kicked him several times in the ribs, breaking three ribs, as well as dislocated his shoulder when they tried to drag his wounded body to the bathroom. They confessed they had hopes of him dying then and where no one could come to his aid. Lucky for him, when he'd been hurt, his family could feel it and alerted someone to come and help him. Damn, but his head still hurt.

"Should you be up and around, young man? I thought you were told to do nothing but lay on the couch for a few weeks. You took a hard blow to—You look a little pale, son. Are you all right?" He told his mom that he'd been bored and had to keep moving, or his wolf was going to take him. "Oh well then. That's good. I know that you can heal yourself, Harman, but those women need to see what harm their actions can do to someone. Would you like me to get you a cup of tea? When was the last time you had a pain pill?"

"I would love a cup of tea so long as you sit with me to drink one yourself." She got busy at the counter, and he sat down. It was his head that was bothering him the most, he told her. Harman told her about the dizziness he was still feeling, too. "I've fallen over a couple of times. And I swear that something is in my ears ringing all the time. But it's my headache that really bothers me. My ribs, too, if I bend too much. Other than that, I'm all right." He wasn't, and the look she gave him told him that she hadn't believed him for a moment.

"I'm going to call the doctor. When I first came in, I did think that you looked a little off. I'll do it now." While she was on the phone, he stayed in the chair. If he was honest with himself, he didn't want to move. He was dizzier with his eyes closed and not moving than he thought possible. Christ, he wanted to shift and get better. "I've spoken to your doctor. He's concerned, and Edwin is going to come over while we wait for an ambulance. He will be better at keeping you steady than I can, I think."

He didn't even argue with her but said he was ready to go. His mom looked as if she'd been crying, and it hurt him that he'd caused it. Trying to talk to her, however got him nowhere. All of a sudden, his brain froze up like an ice cream headache, and it was all he could do to not fall over. Again.

Harman had to close his eyes several times while the medics were there. They were afraid to put him on the gurney they had because he was bigger than the two women who came to get him. It wasn't until two of his brothers, he couldn't focus on who they were, came into the house to help him off the chair and on the gurney that he started feeling sick again.

When they told him he was going to feel a small pinch, Harman thanked them for the meds that he knew would knock him out. Telling his mom that he was better now had her smacking him gently on his arms. Then she sobbed, telling that she loved him with all her heart. And that he needed to know that daily. That was the last conversation they had because it was the good meds he was getting.

It scared him when he woke with a man standing over him with a mask on. He tried to pull his arm free to lash out at him, but he was chained up. Nothing in the world could have prepared him for the fear he had at that moment.

"It's me, Harman. Doctor James. You are at the hospital, and I'm going to send you to surgery to see what we left behind. That's the only thing I can think of that's having you so sick. Even as a wolf and not shifting, you should be feeling better and about healed. You have a hard head, boy." Harman asked where his mom was. And why he was chained to the bed. "She's down the hall. And you're chained up because you've tried to take out a few of my nurses when you're barely awake. Come on now, Harman, just let the meds take you under, and we'll get this taken care of."

He was given more medication, and he felt himself slipping away. Hearing the doctor say that there was an infection scared him enough that he woke fully again. With a nod from Doctor James, he was out again. The meds were finally kicking in.

When he woke again, he was in a pretty room. Harman didn't have any idea why he thought it was pretty. The walls were drab brown, the curtain was a sickly green color that had too many patterns in it, and he could smell every person who had ever been in this room recovering. He looked around when he heard a small sound.

"What's a four-letter word for *fucking*?" Before he could think about it too hard, he told his dad that it was *shag*. "Thank you. It fits. You're awake again. How are you feeling?"

"I don't know? Maybe I'm better? What kind of newspaper has that sort of crossword question in it." Dad laughed and showed him the front cover of the book of crossword puzzles. Then he explained where he'd gotten it. "Mom know that Storm gave you that for helping her out the other day?"

"She thinks it's a hoot. The two of us sit in the living room and, just at random, pick a page and ask each other questions. It's about as much fun as watching television as we've ever had. What do you mean, maybe?" He eyed his dad and realized that his vision wasn't blurry anymore. Haman told his dad.

"How about that noodle of yours? Is it still as painful as it had been?"

"No, now that you mention it. I mean, I'm still in pain, but not like I was at home. This morning?" Dad corrected him. "Three days ago? I really don't care, actually. I do feel a great deal better the more I talk to you. What happened?"

Harman could remember being afraid because someone said infection, but he must have misheard them. But when his dad started explaining what he'd gone through, he was glad that he had been at his parents' home instead of by himself. The doc said that Mom had kept him from dying. He knew that he couldn't, but it could have made him lose some function that his brain needed. Well, he supposed that would be about everything in his body.

He was talking to his dad and sitting up in the second chair in his room when his mom showed up. She hugged him several times, telling him how much he'd scared her and not to do that again. He told her how grateful he was that she'd taken such good care of him. It made him chill a little to think about how close he'd come to having a severe brain injury.

"They found two itty-bitty pieces of red paint from the fire extinguisher in your noodle. I tell you, son, when he showed them to us afterwards, I had a hard time seeing them. But he's what he is, a good doctor because of what he found." Dad wiped his face with his handkerchief, very emotional sounding too. "That's why he makes the big bucks, I guess. Saving my son."

The doctor in question came into the room to talk to him. Telling him what he'd found and that the police had matched it up to the extinguisher that they had in evidence. He could see the tiny specs and, like his dad, was amazed that they'd been found at all. Then he told him his restrictions for when he was in the hospital and when he got home.

"You've had a nasty bump, Harman. Stay down on the couch and let your head rest. No reading, and don't do anything that would cause any kind of strain on your head, face, and neck. I mean this, son. You have to listen to me. And no shifting. I know that will heal you completely, but you and your wolf went through some major trauma, and the two of you must rest." Mom and Dad both promised that he'd stay down even if they had to hog-tie him. "Good. All right. I'm going to keep you one more night, then we'll see about tomorrow. No, why don't we say two nights. Your head looks like it's paining you now, so I'll keep you two nights so that you can get the stronger stuff to keep you down. That way, too, I can keep an eye on you. All right? Any questions?"

No one had any, so he left them there. Mom said that she let the others, the rest of the family, know so that they'd not worry. Haman felt tears fill his eyes when he was emotionally overcome with love for his family. After about ten minutes, he was given the good drug, and his parents left him for home. Harman settled down for a good night's sleep and closed his eyes.

Waking up afraid, he looked around the room. There wasn't anyone in the room that he could smell, so he laid his head back down. The strain, quite a bit of it actually, on his neck hurt him all over. Closing his eyes, he reached out beyond where he was to see if he was the only one up in his immediate area.

The sounds of a woman crying had him listening harder. When that was painful enough, he just listened to her. His mom usually talked to herself when she was upset or happy. This person was silent as the night was around his home. Harman didn't try to search her mind for her problems as his head was paining him again.

~*~

"Oh, Aye then, you try to go on with your life as you

wish. Katie and I will just wait for you to get your head out of your arse and come to the same conclusion the rest of us have. You go on to meet your maker and— You know what, Grannie, how about this? Why don't I drag your skinny arse down to the plot of dirt we just buried your sister in, and you two can go to the pearly gates together? That sounds grand now, doesn't it? Arms around each other and all that. While we are singing and dancing—we'll all do that when you're finally gone on your plot of dirt? How about that? Will you believe us then that she's gone and settle your butt down?" Grannie told her that she wasn't going to speak to her anymore. "You said that yesterday and the day before to myself."

Carrie loved her grannie. But there were times when she wanted to pick her up, give her a good shakin', and put her back. She was ten times the most aggravating person that—not including her cousin Katie. She could wear down a stone with trying to make it move like nobody she'd met before.

A man with a cane entered the room. While she didn't have any idea who he was, he was the most delicious-looking man she'd seen, well, forever. When she saw his face pink up a bit, she grinned.

"You've no right to trespass, ya know that, don't

ya?" He said he was sorry and fumbled around with telling her the reason he'd come into her room. "'Tis my grannie's room, not mine. Yet. She's beginning to wear meself down, and I might be needing a rest before this is all settled. I'm Cassie Donahue, just that, not short for anything. This is my grannie, Catherine Donahue. She's the stubborn one of us all."

"All?" Cassie explained how she'd come to the United States a few weeks ago when her grannie was found at the bottom of the stairs where she'd fallen three days before, just after her sister's funeral. "I'm sorry to hear that. You're very lucky, Ms. Donahue, to have family that will come for you when you need it."

"You'd think that wouldn't ya? Well, I've got something to say about that too. My sister ain't dead. I'm not going to go into one of the hospital places to be wheeled around all the time. I ain't wearing a diaper like some old folks. Nor am I going to wear a big bib and be told like I'm some kind of drunken Irish idiot because I made a shite in my drawers." The man was either shocked to his core or trying hard not to laugh. She thought it was the latter. "Another thing I'm going to say then I won't speak to either of you again, I want a bowl of — not those dainty kind they've been bringing me while here but a bowl of oats that have cooked on the stove like a good and proper oat should be. That'll make them sit up and take some notice when I give them a nice fermenting shite after that. Don't you think, young man?"

He cleared his throat twice before he nodded. "Yes, ma'am, I do think that'll do it. Is there anything that I can get for you? I'm here until the day after tomorrow, and I can get you anything you wish. I've been waiting to get home, and I'm bored again. Not that I think that you're boring or anything, but my mom, who was going to take care of me, was called away suddenly, and she's the only one that—I'm babbling. I do that when I'm embarrassed or confused. I think right now, I'm both. First for—I'll just be quiet now." Grannie asked the young man if he was smooching up to her, and his face went pink again. "No, ma'am. I'm just trying to help you and your granddaughter out."

"If you could see your way to get me some oats that don't have *instant* on the box, I'd be grateful." Grannie looked at her. "Why don't you be dating this kind of man? I believe that he'd give you a good ride or two before you plum wear him out. I would like to have meself a great-great-granddaughter or two before I meet my maker with my hands as empty as they are now."

"You have five, at last count, great-great-grandchildren. You could be snuggling up to them if ye'd not be so flipping aggravating all the time. Joesph is here with his kids come to see you." Grannie told her that they were here for the supposed funeral. "Awe, there's no talking at ya at times. Ya drive me batty."

It was rude of her, but she left the man with her grannie. She was headed to the lifts when he caught up with her. They didn't speak about anything until they were in the lift. She did ask him what floor he was going to and when he asked where the cafeteria was, she said she was headed there to see her cousin as well.

"Why is she having such a hard time believing that your aunt is gone? I'm assuming that she wasn't able to go to the funeral." Cassie told him that she'd been there but was having a bad day. "I'm sorry. That was rude of me to ask. I do hope she gets better."

"She won't. From here, it gets worse by the minute." She asked him what his name was. "I've heard that name before…Canna remember right now, but I know it was something to do with the—" Cassie snapped her fingers. "You're the nursery room man. The one that got them people to show their true colors a few weeks back. It was in the newspaper around here."

"Yes, that's me. And thank you for not saying that I got them fired. I didn't. They did that all on their own." Cassie remembered it now. How the man had been volunteering for the baby section when he'd been hit a few times. Then, a few days later, he'd been brought back into the hospital with an infection. "I should have been home by now, but my mom was called away to help with the death of one of her friend's husband. She would have worried about me if she'd brought me to the house and then left. This is better, anyway. I'm not feeling rushed about getting better. My name is Harman Griffin, by the way. Your grannie is something else."

"Aye, she is at that." They were in the cafeteria when she saw her cousin sitting all alone at one of the tables closest to the windows. It was snowing again, too cold. She'd thought for anything to be out if she were to be asked, but Katie caught the attention of a bird hopping around in the food that had been left out for her. "Grannie is complaining again. I've had enough. It's your turn to talk to her. This here is Harman Griffin. He calmed her down a bit with a promise of steel-cut oats. She's talking up a storm to anyone that isn't us. Have you heard from Joey?"

"She embarrassed me, is what she did." When he

did put out his hand to meet her cousin, Katie didn't take it. In fact, she glared at Harman instead. "I see. I guess rudeness doesn't just run in the elderly part of the family. At least she was good-humored about it." He looked at her. "It was nice to meet you, Carrie. And enjoy the rest of your stay here."

Carrie looked at the good-looking man and then at her cousin. It was true that they didn't know one another all that well. They'd been together when they were both five, but she was carted off to Wales as soon as school started. The two of them talked on occasion, but it was the death of their great aunt that brought her back here with her brother and his family, Joey Donahue.

"You were rude to him." Katie shrugged her shoulders and turned away. "This got something to do with that doctor? The one that made a pass at you?"

"He didn't make a pass at me, and no, my mood lies squarely in Grannie's lap. Why did she have them call us in if she's no mind to listen to what we have to stay about things? I've got more important things to do rather than sitting around here on my ass all the time. Joey, with his four children, is having a better time than I am. And he's stuck in the house with them. Oh lordy, I need a break." When she turned and looked at her, Carrie would have slayed the world for her cousin. She'd helped her enough over the years. "My boss calls. Or my former boss, I guess. He said that I've missed too much work and that I'm not to come back there for any reason. They'll mail my things to me."

"Can they do that?" Katie just looked at her. "Aye, and I ain't from around here now, am I? Just get your panties out of your twist and be nice to me. You know why Grannie refuses to believe why her sister isn't dead?" Carrie sat down on the closest chair and asked her if that was true. "She really believes that her sister is the only one that cared for her. Where she'd get a notion like that, do ya know?"

"I would imagine it has a little to do with her sister dying and her brother blaming it — why do they live to be so old, Carrie? Most of the family is still hanging on after hitting their nineties. You think that Grandda was right in saying that it had to do with the Donahue blood that run rich over the mountains? He's full of malarkey if you were to ask me."

"You have such a pretty way with your wording, cousin. I would have called him a bald-faced liar and been on with my business. You have to pretty it up with 'malarkey' and the likes." Carrie was glad to see the smile on her face. "You're a beautiful woman, Katie, dear. Why are you wasting away over here when there are men around…well, like that Griffin person. He's a sure lot of eye candy if you were to ask me."

"Well, I didn't." Carrie noticed that her cousin did look in his direction but didn't let her gaze linger very long. "Men like him would eat me alive." Carrie told her that would be a nice way to go. "Oh, behave yourself, why don't you. Everything isn't about sex, you know."

"Aye, I know that. I don't believe you do, but therein lies the issues. You're getting to be a dried-up old prune, and that's bad for us Donahue women. You're ruining our reputation by being a old spinster. How old do you be now? Fifty, sixty years old. That sweater that you have on and those ugly shoes tell me that you're that old, at least. Or more. Where is the fancy clothing that all of you Americans wear? You're making me look bad here." Carrie watched her cousin, and when she stiffened, she stepped in front of her. "Aye, I'll be helping you if you wish. We're having a conversation."

"I'm Katie's boss. I want you to…why are you talking like that. You came from the south, didn't you? Some hillbilly or something." Carrie was still trying to figure out why the man thought she was from the south? South of what when he sat down across from her cousin. "I've decided to give you a second chance. You'll come back to work today, and I'll pretend that nothing happened. What do you say?"

Carrie looked at the man, but she was still concerned with her cousin. When Katie stood up and stretched, she thought for sure that she was going to go back to work for the man who had been harassing her for the last several days. She did wonder if this was the reason that Katie was forever in a vile mood.

"No." When she moved away from the table and went to the line that served the people food here, she followed her. There was something going on here, and she wanted to get to the bottom of it before someone, him, she was thinking, got hurt. "What kind of pie did you have before, Carrie?"

Confused, she answered her. "Banana Cream, I think she called it. Best way to use up bananas I've ever heard of. The cherry pie is good, too. Not like Grannie's, but good." The man tried to stop Katie from putting a slice of both pieces of pie on her tray. "Excuse me. What are you talking about?"

"I said that I'm going to take you back despite having more than enough good reason for firing you. You'll have to make up for it by working weekends and overtime. But you'll work hard on things because I'm doing you a big favor right now." Katie asked while not looking at him if he'd figured out her computer was blank. "Yes, and you'll not do that again either. I want your passwords to everything that you do from now on. I'm your boss, and what I say goes, Katie. We'll not be having secrets between us again. Or I will have to terminate you. See that I don't."

"The clients won't work with you. Nor anyone on your staff. While I'll have nothing to do with them leaving your firm, I know for a fact that your daddy will come down on your ass hard if the entire firm closes down because you can't keep your hands and fists to yourself. What do you think he'd say if I brought in the police reports of me having to have you arrested to keep you from raping me? Or the huge hospital bills when you knock me around because I won't have an affair with you." She turned then and looked at the man. For the life of her she couldn't remember his name. A tall shadow slid over her, and she turned to see that Griffin was standing there.

"The lady has given you an answer, and I believe she means it. Why don't you move on to someone that is more your size? Beating on people not necessarily weaker than you but smaller is against the law." Carrie watched as Harman straightened up and looked to be about a foot taller than the man. "Ms. Donahue, if you'd like to beat the crap out of Jimmy here, I'll gladly stand back and make sure he plays fair when you do. He's been a big bully since we were in high school together. Isn't that right, Jimmy boy?"

Jimmy? She didn't think that was right but watched closely as to what was going on. The man only glared at Harman but didn't engage. She did notice that he was puffing out his chest like he was some damned bird or something stepping back when Katie did, she put her hands on her shoulders to let her know that she was there for her.

"What the hell? Are you letting him touch you now, Katie?" The slap startled both men and herself when Katie reddened the cheek of the other man. "What have I told you about hitting me, bitch?"

"Excuse me." Before either of them, Katie or herself could figure out what was going on, Harman had Jimmy in a chokehold and down on the floor just as security came into the vast room. In as little as a few seconds, honestly, Jimmy was being carted off, and Katie and she were left standing there like nothing had happened. Looking around for Harman, he was sitting at his table, looking at the pie that he was forking into his mouth, and didn't turn to look at them. Not even when she said his name. Christ, not only was he good-looking, but he was also a knight in shining armor when someone needed him.

Chapter 2

Sitting at his desk with all his notes in front of him, Harman tried to get his mind where it needed to be to work. He'd been home now for a week, and the only thing he'd gotten finished was his laundry. And he'd not even washed it but had put it away. Having live-in help, he was glad now that he'd hired someone to help, but he was getting no more done than he had before. Figures, he told himself. All this time, he couldn't get his head turned in the right direction.

"Mr. Harman, you have a phone call." He thanked Margaret, and she headed back to the kitchen. Picking up the phone, he decided today wasn't a good day to get bitchy about someone else's habits when he came to phone edict. Knowing who it was helped a great deal, too. When she started talking to him, like she'd had a head start on this conversation just a few seconds ago instead of two hours, he smiled when she cursed, a great deal, as a matter of fact, about people. Humans, he thought. But since she was fully human, too, he wasn't quite sure how that was going to work.

"I'm thinking that I need to hire meself a chemist and have them make a drug that will make ye people smarter. I'm thinking too that you and me, we're the only ones that seem to have the right idea." He asked her what had happened now. "I don't know, but Katie is in a terrible mood again."

He didn't ask if that was any different from any other day of the week but kept his mouth closed. The two of them had butted heads several times in the last couple of days, and he didn't have it in him to get into it with her again.

They talked about the upcoming holidays and what they were going to do. This will be the first time that Carrie and her brother could celebrate the holidays together as they didn't live all that close in Wales. It was doable, but for him, it was too much with children.

"I'm leaving just after Thanksgiving. I was going to stay until the new year, but my momma and sisters want us to come back before that. It's only because I buy the best gifts ever." He thought she might be right on that. He'd been shopping with Carrie and Katie, and Carrie bought gifts from the heart. Katie did as well but it was difficult for him to get close to the other woman as she was forever snipping and biting at him. It was almost too much to hang out with Carrie when Katie was around.

Carrie had been telling him for a couple of days that he should just tell her to shut her trap. His mom would ring his neck if he did that, and he was kinda happy where his neck was at the moment. After telling Carrie that he was going to have dinner with her grannie, she asked him if he was sweet on her.

"I am, as a matter of fact. She's been so nice to me since I was able to get her some good oats. And she tells me that her constitution is a good deal better, too. I love the woman." She laughed and said that the only person she was on the warpath with at the moment was Katie. "What's happened there? Yesterday, you told me that Katie was in her good grace and that you were out again."

"Aye, I was. But she's got a burr up her butt about us leaving soon. Said we've got us nothing there that we can't have here for us." Harman told her that was sad. "It 'tis, it 'tis. She's all alone now when we all go back home. Katie will head home the same day that Joey and I leave. She lives close but not close enough for her to just pop in when she needs her. I don't know why Katie won't stay…Might be because she's out of work right now. Her boss, Jimmy Barnhart, the bastard, he's been calling her daily and showing up at the nursing home since you had him tossed out on his behind."

"I don't think I ever heard what it was that she did for a living. I know that you and Joey run a flower business, but not her." She told him what Katie did, and he was impressed. "So she's that good at being an attorney? Did all his clients leave as she told him that they would?"

Harman looked up when he saw a movement at the door. It was Katie. And she had blood on her face and a nasty bruise on the side of her head that was getting bigger by the second, had him telling Carrie to come over now. It wasn't until then that he noticed that her clothing was all dirty and that there was snow in her hair. Harman called for Margeret.

"Call an ambulance." Katie told him that she'd be fine, but he told Margret that he wanted one now. "Now let me see what damage you did to my front lawn when you fell. Or did you ram your head into the steps? Either way, you're paying for the damages."

"I didn't know where I was when I woke up."

Harman didn't think that was a good thing. "I was wandering around outside when I thought this was your brother's house. If I'm disturbing you, I can go there. Just point me in the right direction. No north or south crap, I don't know my right hand until I pick —" She looked up at him, and he could see that her eyes were glazed over in pain. "I'm sorry if I hurt your sidewalk."

"I think I'll manage." He picked her up from the floor and carried her to the couch. When he got her there, Margaret brought him an ice pack. "Put this on your cheek, and I'm going to inspect your head. I'm going to see if you cut yourself. What happened, if you don't mind me asking."

"I don't know, not really. I was talking to Jimmy, my boss, and telling him not to bother me anymore or I would make his life like he had mine. I remember thinking that there must have been an echo around me when all of a sudden, I felt this incredible pain in my face and then my head." Harman asked what she meant by echo. "Oh, you know when you talk on the phone with someone and it's an echo of what they're saying to you back. That's what I got towards the end of the call. I wonder now if it was that I was in between houses or something like that."

"He was more than likely following you, and that when you turned him down again, he hit you. Nothing that man does here lately surprises me anymore." He found a small hole-like cut on the back of her head and was holding another towel over it when the medics arrived. As soon as he was able to back away from Katie, he went to the door again to let in Carrie and her brother, Joey. Her other brother, Shawn, was there, too. He explained what had happened and told them that he was going to call the police too. "I think he's been following her around for the last few days. When he isn't harassing you, Carrie, he's beating up women."

His brother showed up as well. Edwin came with the police as he'd been at the office talking about the upcoming holidays and how the department was taking donations for the kids' drive. One of the medics showed Edwin the cuts on Katie's head, and Edwin shivered.

"So he's now trying to beat you into submission? This guy isn't very bright if you ask me. This morning, the station was called to the hotel where he's staying. He was demanding someone tell him where you were living." They were lying Katie down on the couch about then, and she said that she had left the hotel to go to the bed and breakfast. Edwin nodded and said that it was probably a better place, but he more than likely saw her leaving the hotel. "If you were trying to keep your move a secret, then I'd suggest that you stay here. No one will get by me as I run a lot of security devices here that I bought. I wrote a book on how to secure your home as a DIY project."

Edwin stared at him and Harman only shrugged at him. *"Is Katie your mate? Or Carrie? Either one of them would be amazing to be related to. Which is it?"*

"I don't know. I've never thought about it. How would I test that out?" Edwin asked him if she smelled good to him. *"I haven't any idea. I've not been able to smell anything since I was born. I told you that."* He looked at his brother and could see the confusion on his face. *"I know that you know. I told everyone at the dinner table one night when we were just kids."*

"Christ, I never remembered that until just now." While Edwin was thinking, or whatever he was doing, with that odd look on his face, Harman watched Katie being worked on. He got a lot of information about her while she spoke to the medics, but could she be his mate? Could Carrie? It was something that he was going to give a lot of thought to when he got home after the emergency room trip that he was going to surely go on. *"Dad wants to know if you can dress and undress*

yourself." He looked at Edwin before telling him that he could do that since he was about two. "*No. I mean —Christ. I mean, when you shift, are you naked when you shift back or not?*"

"*I don't know. I'll try that later. Right now, I'm trying to figure out if I have enough material for a book or two. If there are enough sales then I can pay off the car that I want to buy. Having a mate never entered my mind.*" Harman reached for Katie's hand when she reached for him. He knew that she had to be afraid. He was for her as well.

There was a monster, anyone who beat up defenseless women was a monster, in his opinion, out there gunning for her over a simple job. And that's all it was. Just a job that he'd fired her from in the first place.

As she was put on the gurney, she asked him to bring her sister to the hospital so that she'd not drive. Her brother, as well.

"Sure. I don't know that I'd want to be driving either if my brother had been beaten to shit. I'll bring them back home too if you would just give me a call."

Nodding, she thanked him for helping them out, and she was put in the back of the ambulance. Just as they were pulling out, he and her family loaded up in his truck and made their slippery way to the hospital.

He had not noticed that there had been a heavy snowfall, and it was piling up on the roads and lawns.

It took him less time than he had thought before he was pulling into the parking lot of the ED. As soon as they entered the lobby, he was asked if he was carrying a gun, and he was asked to take it to his car.

"No." He handed them his right to carry as well as his license to say that he worked for the government. He also said that he had to be armed because of his association with the government. "I need to be able to protect myself and those around me. That would include you."

After making a phone call, which was all it took for him to be verified as a government employee and that he'd not been lying about his association with the president, Harman was allowed to not only keep his gun but the knife in his boot pocket as well as the sixteen inches of wire that was wrapped around his wrist in the event he had to up close and personal with someone trying to harm him.

Katie was being prepped for surgery. Like him the second time, they wanted to make sure that they got out any dirt and debris that might have been imbedded into her head from whatever had been used to harm her. When she was wheeled away to the surgical floor, he decided that he was going to go into a bathroom and figure out if he was either of the women's mate. After talking to his brother, his curiosity got the better of him.

He didn't go back with her when she'd been brought up to the unit. Allowing only two visitors, he thought she'd feel better with her family there other than a stranger. But after a few minutes, it was Joey that came out to get him.

"She told me to get you even if I had to drag you in here by your hair. Don't make me have to beg you not to hurt me. Please?" They both laughed. "She's really nervous, and she told me that, for whatever reason, you calm her a great deal."

Another clue that she was either his mate or the cousin's mate. Confused, he entered the prep area and watched as she was having an IV put into her arm. When she reached for him, Harman instinctively kissed the back of her hand after taking hers into his much larger one.

It was all he could do not to cry like a child. Every part of his body started to tingle, and he knew on some level that this was normal. He had claimed his mate. Lying his head on the bed beside her, he let it roll over him in large, painful waves. Harman knew that Katie was hurting too, but it was all he could do to make sure that he didn't shift while waiting for whatever happened to be finished.

He woke up lying on the bed beside Katie. It was the biggest hospital bed that he'd ever seen, and he was glad that someone had thought of that when they'd put him here. Looking around, he saw his brother, Edwin, as well as his wife, Storm, in the room. He asked where they were.

"Hospital still. She's had her surgery and got about two hundred stitches in the back of her head as well as on her back. I'm assuming that you didn't notice those." He told Storm that he'd not. He was more concerned with her head. *"I can see that. She's going to be just fine, thanks to you claiming her. I'm wondering if you can smell now. No biggie if you can't yet, but it's something that I'm curious about."* Harman leaned over to Katie and inhaled deeply. He could not only smell her, but he knew that she was ovulating. After telling Storm that, she nodded. *"I figured as much. All right. Some things that you should know before she wakes up. Her boss is in jail. I wish I would have found him first, or we'd not have to worry about someone getting him out. But there is still time for that."*

"You may think that's comforting, but it's not.

You scare the shit out of me when you say things like that. Especially in that soft voice that you have." She laughed, and he smiled. *"What else. Whatever it is, can it wait? I'm all right, but my wolf isn't. He's feeling pissy with me. Is that normal?"*

"Is there anything about you Griffin men that is normal? Don't answer that. I know the answer without you telling me." He laughed again and turned to see that Katie was staring at him. *"I'm going to leave you two when I tell you both what has been going on. Most of it you might have already guessed, but I'll let her know as well.*

After telling the two of them what had been going on, Storm and Edwin left. Edwin said that he'd come by later with some food but wouldn't stay. He figured that they had a lot to talk about. Think about as well.

Once they were alone, he sat up slowly and looked down at her. After getting up and stretching so that his wolf was able to do the same, he sat down in the chair Edwin had been in after moving it closer to the bed. Taking her hand into his. He again kissed the back of it as he leaned into her.

"I'm sure you have questions. I do, too." She told him she had too many to put in order right now. "I'm good at sorting through your answers if you want to shot gun the questions to me. Right now, I'm feeling good, but I know that you're not. You know what happened, I'm assuming. Since you didn't freak out when you saw me lying next to you in the bed."

"I guessed that you were my mate." He corrected her. "What's the difference in whose mate is whose? It can't be that big of a deal for you to be mated to me or the other way around. We're still mates when you get to the end of the day."

"By me saying that I belong to you, I'm telling you that you will forever command me. I would die for you if I could and move heaven and earth to make sure that you're as happy as you can be. It's my duty, something that I really would like to do, to do whatever you want of me. And this is about as truthful as I can say to you, I would take a bullet for you. Again, you nor I will ever die, but it's—" She asked him what he meant when he said they'd never die. "We're immortal, the two of us. I've been around for centuries and centuries. My entire family has been. My dad is the first generation of shifter wolves that were—"

"Wait, wait, wait. You're telling me that you're an ancient being that won't ever die? And through our association, whatever you want to call it, I won't die either. I don't know if I like that idea or not. I mean, I have family around that I'd just as soon not outlive me. I know that sounds cold, but I love my family. Even if they irritate the crap out of me." He told her that they'd not die either. "So you can what? Sprinkle faerie dust on them, and they're immortal, too? What about their children? And their children's children? What happens when we populate the entire world with Donahue's?"

He couldn't help but throw back his head and laugh. Harman hadn't laughed this hard in…well, he didn't have any idea how long it had been. But he was delightfully giddy with his mate and wondered if they all had this much fun when they found each other. She asked him if he was finished making fun of her.

"I'm not, I promise. I love you, believe it or not. And you've made me feel better than I have in some time." He kissed the back of her hand again and stared at her. "Christ, where have you been all my life?"

"Not born yet." That made him laugh, too. "You keep that up, and they're going to lock you away from everyone. Then where will I be? I will admit this: You do calm me. Is that supposed to happen?"

"Yes. You calm my beast as well." She asked who his beast was, and he explained to her what he meant. "So you call your wolf a beast. How does he take that? I don't know that I'd be all that thrilled to be called a beast."

"You're right. But I've never asked him before. Or even thought about how he might feel. There are times when I think that he is a separate being from my other half. It's odd, but when he's out, he makes decisions that I wouldn't dare to make. Nothing terrible but just doing things on his own mind." She told him he was weird. "I guess I am."

~*~

Harman left her for a while after supper was given to them. Edwin stayed with her, talking small talk that she abhorred when she finally had enough and asked him what he wanted to say to her. When he grinned, she thought that he could pass for Harman's twin. They looked so much alike in that moment. However, to believe that he was as old as Harman said that they were boggled her mind.

"You're thinking too hard. I can almost taste your confusion." She said that she was but didn't know how to get to the bottom of it. "That's all right. It's a great deal to get used to. But as you were told by Harman, you have plenty of time, and anything that is going on, it's something that you can work out or just go with the flow. However, I don't think you're a go-with-the-flow sort of person."

"Not particularly. It's a great deal to be thrown at me, as you said. The plenty of time has me coming back to that over and over. As I was talking to Harman, he said that my family would be around, too and their offspring. At what point does that become too much? At some point, it's going to be too much. Correct?" He told her that it wouldn't really. "How so?"

"My parents are talking about having their immortality taken from them. They're tired and have seen enough that they're wanting to fade away. They don't die, just fade away. With that, they can talk to us and guide us but not be around. It's up to them, but I know that I'd miss having them around. Same with the others." She asked him what happened when someone didn't want to have immortality?" It was then that Harman came back, and he answered her.

"Sometimes it's just safer to not give someone immortality. Like if someone has been a real bastard to their family, they will not receive it. It would be entirely up to you on who you want to hang around with you for eternity." He kissed her on the lips and then sat down. "I'm not as antsy as I was before. I needed some fresh air. I've never been able to smell or taste things before and the smells in the hospital here are just too much for myself and my other half. See how I did that?

I didn't call him a beast. But I feel better now. I guess that's something else I'll have to get used to. It's not that I'm complaining, but it's different for me."

"You couldn't smell or taste?" He told her that it had been that way since he'd been born. "I can't imagine not being able to smell things. Nor taste them. The thought of all that you missed just in taste makes me sad and sorry for you. If nothing else comes of this relationship but that, I'd be happy."

"Thank you." He smiled at her, and her heart did a little flip-flop. When his brother cleared his throat, they both turned to look at him. Edwin said that he had to go. After he left them, they dug into their dinner and she was laughing so hard when Harman told her about the tastes of each item on his sub. It was like an awakening for him. To be able to taste things, she was sure he was going to someday soon find something that he didn't care for, and she wanted to be there when— looking at him, with her sub halfway to her mouth, she realized something. He asked her what was going on.

"How can I be in love with you so fast? I mean, I know that you and I have been around each other for the last month but why now am I feeling that I can't live another day without you there for me?" He said that he felt the same way about her. "But I'm just a plain human. I've no special talents, nor do I howl at the — Do you do that?"

"We do. When we have a pack meeting, and it's a full moon." She asked him if he was joking with her. "No. I'm serious. Also, you should know that I can never lie to you. Not that I'd want to, but I can't. I won't cheat on you, ever. My heart and body belong solely to you. And you should also know that you're no longer just a plain human. From the moment that I claimed you, with the kiss to your hand, you became more of everything."

"Like what? Can I shift with you?" He told her no, not that he'd been made aware of. "Well, that sucks. I was thinking that it would be fun to be another half of myself. To run through the woods and chase my tail, so to speak."

"Let me rephrase that for you. I don't *know* if you can or not. There is a great deal of magic in this family, not even counting what I gave you that you might well have inherited from Storm and Rain. They're the most powerful beings ever created." She asked him why them. He explained about how his father came to be the holder of the magic.

"I know that you can't lie to me, but I find that hard to digest. Right now, anyway." He told her that was understandable. "All right. Is there anything else that I have to know right now? I'm all of a sudden exhausted, and my head hurts a little. I'm sure that you have something to do with that, but I'm exhausted from thinking about things, too. I'll sleep, and you watch over me."

"It would be my pleasure." As she snuggled down into the covers, she realized that she wasn't going to sleep alone. Her body and mind had gotten used to, even after one night, having his big, warm body around her, and she needed it again. She only had to open the covers up, and he laid down with her.

She had expected a nasty or even a funny remark, but he only got into the bed with her. As she wrapped herself around him, she laid her head on his chest. As she listened to his heart beating, just a soft thud in his chest, she closed her eyes. Katie was asleep in minutes.

Waking up with the sun shining through her window, she was disappointed to find that she was alone in the big bed. Sitting up, she was thrilled to find a note from Harman on the landline phone that was next to her. Opening it to read it, she couldn't believe his handwriting. It was elegant and beautiful. Reading the note, she had to work hard at not sobbing.

"I've been called away for a couple of days. This

is a government job, so I will have to wait until I return before I can share it with you. Sometimes, they'll call me in for stupid things, but this one is going to take me a few days. Call Edwin or any one of my other brothers to take you to my house when released. Next time, I'll take you with me." Then he signed it with 'love, H.'

Not at all sure what to do, she was both happy and a little stressed when Storm showed up — popped in, she called it — to answer any of her questions. As they sat there, Storm talked to her about some of the things she was able to figure out. Katie found that she liked the other woman and was glad for her help.

"Also, your boss, Jimmy Barnhart, was in jail, but he's out now. Not that you have to worry about him. No one can enter the houses with ill will in their hearts. Meaning the need to harm you. But that's all there is about him. He'll either keep pushing until he ends up dead or not. I could care less." Katie said that she felt the same way about him. "Also, I have it on good authority that he'd been given four weeks' notice to get the office straightened out, or he's going to be fired. That's from his own father. I don't think they like each other."

"They don't. There was a falling out about four years ago. Jimmy caused a big ruckus at the offices by sexually harassing the male employees. I could care less as it meant that he was leaving me alone, but he suddenly became interested in me when I started winning cases. His father and I are on good terms. Maybe I should give him a call and tell him what's going on." Storm handed her the cell phone that suddenly appeared. "That's something else I'm going to have to get used to, isn't it?"

"I would say that is a good thing, don't you? However, after a couple of days, you more than likely won't notice it. You'll just take it in stride, and that'll be fine, too." They both laughed. "Call Jimmy Barnhart, senior, and tell him what had happened. Including how you were here for the funeral of your aunt and your grandmother became ill. Tell him too that you're in the hospital for what he did to you. I know that he's the one that did it. His thinking was if you were dead, his dad could no longer be upset that he can't seem to get you to come back to work for him. That's the most idiocy thing I've ever heard of, but criminals are pretty stupid."

"That I can agree with you on. I had a lot of stupid criminals when I was working." She asked her what she did. "I was an attorney for Barnhart and Barnhart. I did my internship there and stayed after I passed my boards. It was a nice family-owned practice, and I liked the people that, well most of the people that I worked with. Jimmy was the worst, but he didn't come into the office all that often, so it was easy to avoid him. Besides, I think he is gay, and that is something that his father knew about before Jimmy had."

"Figures. I've heard of that happening a great deal with older men who come out. Good for him, I guess, but sexual harassment is sexual harassment no matter what way you swing."

When he called the personal number of Jimmy's senior cell phone, she was glad when he told her that he had heard that she'd been hurt. He told her that he wanted to visit with her as soon as possible. He was going to be at her room in the hospital first thing in the morning. She couldn't wait. It was high time that someone took Jimmy to task.

Chapter 3

Jimmy was tired of the cell he was in. They wouldn't allow him to have any music or the snacks that he had all over his apartment when he was home. He had made sure that when he hired his cook, she knew to keep the snack food around where he could get to it at any time. After three tries, him knocking her around after each failure, she finally got it right.

He wasn't sure, however, but he thought that she was putting holes in the bags he was getting. Some of the things, like the white cheddar popcorn that he would munch on, would be stale. He'd not confronted her about that just yet, but he was going to do so as soon as he got home. Being in jail and without his cell phone made it very difficult for him to keep up with his daily life. He was going to talk to someone about having cell phones and chargers in the cells for entertainment. They didn't have to be completely savage about keeping people behind bars.

"You have a visitor. Would you like to talk to them back here or in one of the observation tanks?" He asked the cop who it was. "I don't ask for identification when someone comes in and wants to see you. I just ask if you want to see them or not."

"Then how am I supposed to know if I want to see them or not if I don't know who it is?" The man simply opened the door for him. "What happens if it's someone that I decide that I don't want to see? What happens then?"

"Do you want to see them or not? I don't have time to go around wiping your ass every time something happens. Yes or no?" He didn't understand that logic either but decided it would be nice to look at another four walls rather than the ones he'd been looking at for two days. "Good for you. It's your father."

Christ, Jimmy would have talked to anyone but him. However, he was nearly to the closed door that separated him from freedom, and he really did want to be out of the cell. Usually, he was forever on the move. Making plans and closing deals. Sitting with his father meant that he was going to be lectured again, and he didn't want to have his good mood burst because of something that his dad was for sure going to say to him.

As soon as he was seated, they actually put his cuffs through the large ring on the table. It was something that he'd been thinking about having as well. Put it on his desk so that when the underlings came into his office, they'd have to sit there until he released them. He also thought that it would make an awesome sexual toy too. Just thinking about it had him hard as stone.

"Well, you've screwed the pooch, haven't you, Jimmy? You couldn't just let her have the time off that she needed when she needed it, and now we're losing the best-damned attorney that I've ever met. Including myself." He asked about him. "You and I both know the only way that you were able to pass your boards is because you paid someone to take the test for you. If they ever find out—perhaps I'll tell them after this, but when they find out, I'm going to have a good time telling you that I told you so. Why did you fire Katie Donahue?"

"You know as well as I do why I terminated her. She missed a month of work." His dad asked him if that was all. "No. But if I tell you, you're not going to be any happier with me. I don't like her for one thing.

She's forever correcting me on things. Did you know that the state of Texas has a law about homosexuals?"

"Everyone of the states as far as I can remember, has laws. Whether or not they follow them is up to the abuser. What sort of law are you talking about?" He told him. "I wasn't aware that you were planning on getting married to someone. When did this happen?"

"I'm not getting married to anyone. I like my freedom too much. No, what I was saying is that I could if I wanted to. Did they have those same laws when you were growing up?" He told him he wasn't gay, so he didn't realize that there were laws that he'd have to look into before marriage. "But you could now if you wished. That's what I'm talking about with her. She's forever saying shit like that and backing it up even with the law books that she'd read it in. Isn't that the most annoying thing ever?"

"Why would you think that's annoying, son? She's a good attorney. The best. And I'm proud of her for knowing laws like that one. I'm sure she knows plenty more, too, if asked. You fired her because she's smarter than you? Hell, Jimmy, the cleaning crew, more than likely knows more than you do about the law. Why would you...you know what? I don't care. I'm sure that in your emptily packed head from lack of law information could fill all the books in the world." He didn't understand that, so he didn't comment. It was just like his father to talk over his head when he was with him. "Did you know that she's going to work for the Griffin family? I'm sure you remember who they are. We just talked about them a couple of months ago."

"Remind me." After rolling his eyes, his dad told him what they'd been talking about. "So she's jumped ship with us to go and work for them? Is it because of the money? I could try to get her back by offering her more than they are. Will that make you happy? I realize that when you're happy, I can be happy. It's our yin and yak sort of part we play in each other's lives."

"No. And it's yin and yang, not yak. What would make me happy is if you were to get your head out of your ass and think about the lack of impact you're making on the lives of those people that are working for you. Or I should say *were* working for you." He asked his dad what he meant by that. "I'm too old to go back to work as an attorney because you've made a mess of things. It hurts me that after I close up, there will be no more Barnhart and Barnhart Attorney at Law. I have a meeting tomorrow with not only Katie but also the head of the Griffin family. I'm going to sell them not just my firm name but let any of the others there go to them if they wish. I'm sick of picking up the pieces weekly when you're being paid to work. Then, in a couple of months, after they're well established — not that I see it taking that long for them to be working at having their own clientele, they'll drop my name, and I'll be finished with it all. Thank the good lord for that too. At least my family's legacy will be attached to a good name rather than the one that it currently has that you did to us."

"How much are they going to pay me? As much as they are Katie, I'm thinking. I'm a Barnhart and am immensely more important to the firm than she is." He told him that he wasn't a part of the deal. "Why not? What the hell am I supposed to do without you paying me weekly? I do have monetary needs, Father. Or do you want me to move back home with you and Mom and…You know, that has merit. I think living at home would be the best thing for me. Then, when you both are dead, I can just slip into the role of reigning king and have it all."

"Reigning king? Christ, Jimmy, you're barely a blip on my radar of you taking over my home and money. Your mother and I have plans with our savings, and believe it or not, you are not included." He told his dad that he was simply being too mean to him. "Good. Also, I've decided that you no longer need some of the perks you had as the person running the law firm. The car, credit cards, expense account as well as your suits aren't going to be something that you can rely on any longer. You'll no longer be able to charge large lavish meals to the company. I have a list of things that I'm to take care of before you're released from here." As his dad dug things out of his pocket, Jimmy kept thinking that this was an April Fools joke. Although it was neither the first of the month, it wasn't even April. But that had to be it. "Here it is. I'm to change the locks on the homes that we own. Make sure to run an ad in the newspaper saying that I'm no longer going to be responsible for your debt. She told me that I should send out a letter too just to make sure that everyone is aware of that."

"Who told you to do this?" He snatched the long list out of his dad's hand and looked it over. When his dad took it back from him, Jimmy was shocked. "That is Katie's handwriting. Why are you getting a list from her on how to treat me? I won't tolerate you allowing her to have you treat me this way."

"Well, that's just too damned bad. Your mom and I have talked it over, and we're not going to continue supporting you for the rest of our lives." He told his dad to turn things over to him now. "You'll be broke by the end of the year and wonder what happened to it all. No. We've rewritten our will and have put our house on the market. Katie is making arrangements for us to dissolve the ownership of the houses that we have here and abroad. It's the best decision that I think your mother and I have ever made. That and falling in love."

"What about when I was born?" Dad just stared at him. "Christ, that's harsh of you. Didn't I ever mean anything to you two?"

"Not since you were in high school and hurt that young man because he wouldn't have sex with you." His dad's voice had turned hard when he said that, and there was a little bit of fear rolling over himself. "I didn't care, and still don't, if you're green and purple, Jimmy. Your coming out was fine with us so long as you were happy. But you continued and continued to do things to other people simply because you wanted something and they weren't giving it to you."

"I don't understand what the problem is with that. You've always told me to get what I wanted no matter how." His dad rephrased what he'd said. "Whatever. I don't like that you're going to be giving me stipulations now that you think that I never worked for the things that I wanted. I did work. Do you think it was easy for me to make people do things for me? Not even Katie would do anything unless I knocked her around a bit beforehand. Now, all of a sudden, she's better than I am? No. I don't want that. You change things back to what they were before, or I'll not speak to you for the rest of your life."

Dad started laughing. At first, it was just a spurt or two of laughter. Then he stood up, buttoned his coat, and laughed harder. Every time he sounded like he had some control over his mirth, he would look at him and start anew laughing. Jimmy thought he was deranged by the way he had to keep stopping to lean over and laugh. It was almost like he didn't care if he spoke to him again or not.

But that couldn't be right. He was his son. The one that would carry on—well, he'd not carry on his name for him. The thought of having children running around him was just too much to think about. Shivering, he was taken back to his cell to think.

If his father actually did what he said he was going to do, Jimmy didn't know what he'd do. He couldn't see his father just simply disowning him. Because that was what it sounded like to him, he was going to do. But that couldn't be right. Who would he leave things, especially all his money, to if it were not for him? The longer he sat there, thinking about what his dad had said, the more he realized that his dad had been just been lecturing him and making him nervous. But it wouldn't work. Not at all. He was onto him now.

By the time he had his dinner brought to him, he was thinking about the things that he was going to do when he moved into the house with his parents. First and foremost, there weren't going to be rules on him about having parties at the house. Nor was he going to be left out in the cold because they only had one limo service. As his son, he should have his own limo when he went out and came home. That would also take care of the fact that he'd lost his driver's license three months ago and wasn't to drive anymore. Not that it stopped him, but he was going to use that to make his dad give him his own service.

He wished that he'd asked his dad about food service here, too. Opening his dinner up that had only just then arrived, he was dismayed to find that all he had was a slab of meat, some green beans that looked to be overcooked, as well as a large flop of mashed potatoes that had some kind of greasy looking stuff in the small bowl that had been mashed into them. He looked at the list on his tray and read it over.

"Reg food. No allergies." He asked himself what reg food was and surmised that it had to be reggae food. "Doesn't look like anything I've ever seen in the islands. What the hell is this crap? A bottle of water? Who drinks water nowadays? No one, that's who."

After tasting the mashed potatoes, he decided that they weren't horrendous. But the gravy, what he'd read on the sheet with his meal said it was, wasn't his cup of beer, seeing the line of grease that was on its middle part. No way was he eating that. And meatloaf? What the fuck kind of concoction were they trying to poison him with?

In the end, he ate everything on his plate, including using his bun to get more gravy in his mouth. After he taste-tested the green beans, he decided that if all vegetables tasted like them, he'd gladly just eat them. But the best was the meatloaf.

He knew there was no way he'd ever eaten such a weird and strange food. Then he, purely by accident, he'd mixed some of the gravy with the potatoes. It had to all be eaten together to make the awful potatoes rise up, and it would be wonderful if you ate it with gravy on it.

The meatloaf was meaty and moist. Loving the

crispy tomatoey edges that he'd discovered when a bit of them had gotten into his mouth. It nearly had him begging for more of just that. As he finished off his plate of food, he discovered that there was some sort of pie, too.

Even after getting the meatloaf eaten, he was still leery of the pie. Scrapping off the top layer of the fluffiest stuff off it, he nibbled around it on his fork. Finding that it wasn't so bad, he took a bite of the creamy filling. The banana flavor took his breath away and nearly had him picking up the whole pie, creamy stuff on top and all right into his mouth so that he could enjoy it.

It took him less time to figure out what the pie was than it did his meatloaf. He'd been sure that it was the brown liquidity stuff on his potatoes and not the loaf. It was banana cream with meringue. Jimmy wanted it on everything that he ate from now on. When they came to get his tray, against his better judgment, he asked if he could have a second helping. The man, this time, told him that his wife had made it for them tonight, and he'd get right on that for him.

After twenty minutes, time enough for him to think that he wasn't coming back, he was brought not just another tray of food, but the cop had also thrown in some cornbread, another thing that he'd never eaten before that had been left over from lunch today.

"There's honey and butter if you want to smother it all over your bread. The best way to have it is dripping in it." When he was alone, Jimmy ate his dinner almost too quickly and looked at the cornbread. He was just trying to figure out how one went about smothering something onto a thick slice of bread when he was told that it would be an hour when it would be lights out.

Jimmy was full, too much so, but he was going to try the cornbread. It was like he'd been asleep for years, and this was his first meal that he'd been given. He'd never had such wonderful food and hoped that tomorrow's menu was just as good. While he did like the cornbread, he didn't love it like he had the meatloaf. He could really get used to this if he had to stick around much longer.

~*~

"Mistress, he seems to be in a much better mood than he was when he was first arrested. It's because of the food." Katie, still getting used to having the little faerie named Ice Cream around her all the time, asked him what was so special about the food. "He is tasting things that he'd never had before. When the jail tender came back for the second tray, he went on and on about how delicious the meatloaf was. I've no idea what that is, but he seemed to think that it was the best thing with honey and butter all over it. I would dearly love the honey myself, but I've never eaten the other."

"I'll have someone make it for you next time we're at home. I think he'd put the honey and butter on his cornbread and—never mind." He thanked her but told her to not to go to so much trouble for just him. "I love cornbread. My mom used to make it when ends were hard to meet. It would fill you up with some soup beans, and I'd be full all day."

"I would like that, I think." She asked him why they had been asked to come to this building. "Oh, yes, your question. There is a vampire that lives deep into the building. He's very old and in need of a more secure place to rest. By resting, I mean during the hottest part of the day for him. He is a good friend of the elder Griffin and his wife, Queen Luna. They're the magical world's favorite magical couple for all they've done for our kind and so many others."

"All right. He won't bite me, will he? I mean, should I have garlic around me or something?" A voice deep in the darkness told her that garlic no longer affected him. "Oh, you can hear me. I'm sorry. This is my first assignment for the family."

"You are doing well. Come into the building so that I might have a look at you, my dear. You've nothing to fear from me. My name is Alexander Smith. I am but a humbled vampire that is down on my luck." She told him that she doubted that he was very humble and smiled. "Ah, a woman trying to win my favor. It's been so long. But to be visited by the mate of Harman Griffin makes me feel like a new man. Thank you for coming."

For the next hour they sat at a table that Ice Cream made for the two of them to use. She had paperwork for him to look over and some things to sign. As an acting attorney for the Griffins, she was able to show him the things that were a benefit for him. As well as point out some of the things that he should be made aware of so that his estate would be safe.

"I gave this information to Edwin just yesterday. For you to have found all my property is a wonder. Some of the items that are on this list are ones that I'd forgotten about over the years. Thank you for that." She told him that she was glad to be able to help him. After getting his affairs in order, she showed him the things that Harman and herself were doing for him. Mostly, it was to give him the house that he'd been living in and making it clear that he was able to stay with them in their finished basement if he needed a safer place. "I cannot thank you enough for that. I find, however, that I grow weary of people and would like to end my life on my own terms."

"You feel like you have nothing more to live for? That's sad. But I don't blame you." She smiled at him. "Did Harman tell you that he could taste and smell now? He'd never been able to do that before. He takes his time, smelling the roses, so to speak. I can't imagine what it must have been like to have no sense of smell or taste. And now, a whole new world of things had opened up for him. Simply because he met me. Wouldn't that be grand if I could give you the same motivation? I know that I have stopped what I was doing a great deal more to smell the flowers around me." She looked at her paperwork, slightly embarrassed about her going on and on. "You must think that I'm a silly romantic."

"I don't think you silly at all. However, I would classify you as a romantic. Are you, by chance, telling me in your own way that I need to stop and smell the things around me?" She felt her cheeks heat up, and she looked at him. "Oh, my dear. Does Harman yet know what a treasure he has in you? How you are the best thing that has ever happened?"

"He doesn't often enough, I don't think. But I have no trouble reminding him to remember that." The large vampire threw back his head in mirth. It made her giggle when she realized that he was surprised by the humor and that he now had a small glint in his eyes that hadn't been there before.

After they were finished up with everything, she was in no hurry to get up and leave and they had an enjoyable extra hour where they talked about things that were going on around town. Little and large, Alexander was happy that she had some information on the things.

"So the mayor is on his way out, you say?" She told him how they'd figured out he was taking money from other departments to put into his own personal accounts. "To cover his mother-in-law's gambling debt. Oh, the things we do for family at times. She more than likely goes right back out after he pays things off so that she can gamble again. It's a sickness, you know. One that some vampires get too deep in and their entire lives work is taken from them."

"Have you ever gambled? Even if it was just a small bet?" He said that he hadn't, but he knew many others, humans too, that ended their lives when it got to be too overwhelming. "I understand that. I had a client who was into gambling so bad that he lost not only his entire business but his home, family as well as his reputation. It's sad when the only way out of something like gambling is to take your own life. It's been like that for years, I think. The way that the disease affects so much of your life." She began picking up her things so that she could leave the gentleman to his rest.

"Darling child, I have so enjoyed spending the afternoon with you. I'm not even sorry that I took up so much of your time that you could have been spending with others." She told him that she was new to the family, and they had asked her to help out. "Good for them. They're a good lot. I love Edwin to pieces. He's saved my life a couple of times. Just to give me a place to hide and sometimes heal had made me indebted to the entire family."

Standing up when he said that he must rest, she asked if she could give him a hug. Before she allowed him to answer her, she pulled him into her arms and held him tightly. When he finally returned her hug, she looked up at him when they were both satisfied.

"You must hang around for a bit longer, Alexander. I would love for you to meet my cousins. Joey and Carrie are heading back home in a few days, and Carrie will forever love meeting you. They would never tell anyone, never that, but it would be something that they'd treasure for a long time." He told her that he'd enjoy that as well. "Good. Tomorrow night, come to the house after dinner. Or before, I don't care so long as I can show off my new friend."

"Do you think of me as your friend, Lady Katie?" She said she did. It didn't matter if he didn't think of her in the same way, but he was her friend forever, no matter what path he took in the future. "My, but you are a charmer. And the thing is, I believe every word you've said to me is the truth. Thank you."

He kissed her on the cheek, and she smiled at him. After he walked her to the door in which she came in, she made her way home. It was the best time she'd ever had as an attorney, and she really was going to treasure the time she'd spent with him for a long time.

The house was empty when she got there. There were several envelopes with her name on them on the table in the front hall. Picking them up, she made her way to the dining room, her makeshift office for now, and opened them. The first one surprised her. It was her marriage license to Harman. The note said that it had been filed, but that didn't mean that she couldn't have a nice big wedding at a later date. The next was the paperwork that she'd filed on behalf of Edwin this morning. The deed for the house that he'd given Alexander was ready to be filed.

"Are you busy?" She told Rain that she wasn't. *"Good. I'm going to pop in. I have some questions that I need, as a legal bagel…that sounded funnier in my head. Anyway, I'm on my way."*

Appearing in the room with her, Rain snapped her fingers and sat down. There was a beautiful pot of something in front of her, as well as two of the most beautiful tea cups she'd ever seen. However, she thought that she couldn't enjoy them for the look on Rain's face. She looked stressed.

"I have some news." She said that she'd listen to her. "Thank you. It's very kind of you to…You know, I'm going to just come out with it. Did you know that your boss senior and his wife are moving away? I know that you're going to sell off their homes for them when you're licensed here — you already are, just so you know. You have a license to work anywhere you want to set up shop. I did that for you. Storm will be jealous because she didn't think of it first, and I'm happy about that."

"You're beating around the building. Tell me what it is you're stalling about. And so you know, I thought I heard that you two were straight shooters and that I'd have to get used to the two of you telling me like it is." Rain smiled at her and sipped her tea. "All right. My old boss is moving away with his wife. Why should I be concerned with that? I'm assuming that's what you mean."

"Yes. They're going to die. Soon after leaving the States." She asked if she could stop that from happening to a nice couple. "No. I'm afraid not. If they're set to die, then they will. It'll be some other way and more horrific than it was before. No, it's just best to let that one go and pick up the pieces when asked. They have no heir. Not to say they don't have anyone they can leave things to, but they're going to soon write Jimmy out of the will that they both have. You can't help with that either. It's better, actually, if you don't."

"Why?" Rain took another sip of tea, but this one seemed to be longer than necessary. "What are you... they're going to leave it to me, aren't they? I don't want that?"

"Yes, they are, and yes you do. That's why I'm here. So that when you find out, you're going to use their estate to help others. A lot of others." She said she had enough money of her own to do that now. "No, you don't. Their estate is large and well-established. They're going to also, as you know leave you with the firm too. I'm going to help you a little with some of the charities that would make them happy. But I also think, and I'm not telling you to, you need to help Jimmy."

"With their money? No, I won't do that either. If they didn't want him in the will…again, I think you've not told me everything. Why are you giving it to me in bits and pieces?" She told her. "I guess I can understand that. You don't see the entire picture just yet, but you know that it's going to be necessary for me to help Jimmy. All right. I'll keep an open mind about that. What else do you know? Anything bad?"

"I'm sorry, but it's going to be the manner in which Jimmy needs your help. I can't see it all, but it's worse than I had first thought." She put her hands over Rains when she closed her eyes. "He's not a good man. Not even if you were to take some of his traits away that he's been relying on since he became an adult. He's using people. Regardless of whether they realize it or not, Jimmy continues to use people up until they have no choice but to end their lives. It's as harsh and surreal as that. He then simply steps over them and goes to the next fool that said that they'd help him."

"He never used me." She told her because she was smart enough to not allow it to happen. And that it wasn't for lack of trying on his part. She told her to think about it. Closing her eyes, she thought about the times he'd come to her asking for help. She looked at Rain then. "He wanted me to help him find a date for him for a party that he was attending."

"Yes, that's just one. He thought that he'd be able to convince you to go with him, a show of support he told you, but you turned him down. He would have killed you that night. As it was when he wrecked his car, killing two people in a crosswalk. You would have been murdered by him later that night because you'd not lie that he'd had nothing to drink." She thought of other times that he'd come to her for a date to something. Katie knew that he was a homosexual and often wondered why he'd ask her to go. "He needed to maintain the presence that he was a regular guy — his thoughts to call it that, not his fathers — so that they'd not lose any clients that might be too set in their ways to climb on the LGBTQ community that they served."

She just stared at Rain. "Right now, I have a long list of things that he asked me to do for him. All of them that I can think of had something to do with a crash or trouble that he ended up in afterward. He even blamed some of them on me, telling me that I should have been with him and he'd not have done whatever he'd done to get into trouble." It made her hair dance on her skin when she thought hard about it all. "I'm either very lucky, or someone was watching over me all this time."

"I believe that you've been watched over too. Not only that, but you know what is right or wrong, and you just went with your heart. The only thing that saved you." Katie asked her what she needed to do now. "Nothing. You know as much as I do now, and I'm glad that you do. Whatever befalls you from now on, you'll be smarter in taking care of it simply because you're aware."

"Thank you." She nodded and watched as Rain's mood turned around. "Now you're in a good mood. After telling me that I could have died? That's just not right."

"Remember, you're alive. You must keep telling yourself that you are here and now, with Harman in your life, because you are a smart cookie."

Chapter 4

Harman didn't feel like he was getting anywhere on the book he was trying to put together. He had, long ago, made himself a flowchart that would keep him on track when writing but he couldn't for the life of him start the first chapter. He'd started over just today on the book fourteen times only to get about a thousand words in and then delete it all.

He'd decided a couple of days ago that he was going to write about the babies being born in the hospital, but when he sat down at his desk, there was nothing in his head but cobwebs and empty spaces. Today when he'd gotten into his chair, he did the same thing and hadn't even a single word toward the beginning of the first chapter.

Christ, he felt like he had — pulling out his notes that he'd been taking at the hospital after he'd been nearly killed, he read over what he wrote to himself about the women. They'd been working there for a long time, and he'd surmised, but it was him being in there that brought home how much he disliked them. And their ways of putting people and their families into two categories.

They were either road trash—he didn't quite understand that one, or they were blinking the system by having too many kids. Over the two weeks that he'd been working there, he knew just about all he could stand to know about everyone who had given birth over that time period, as well as any employee who didn't work the day they were talking about them. These women were brutal, too. The nurses had taken their anger—why anger? He couldn't have said—and pointed it right at him. After he lectured them about the similarities between themselves and the people they were talking about it was then that one of them picked up the fire extinguisher and began hitting him in the head with it. Several times, as it turned out.

Leaning back in his chair, he stared at the computer screen. It was right there, just on the outer edges of his brain, to write a book. This one was entirely different than he'd ever written before. Usually, he wrote about flower gardens and what to plant when.

Volcanic ash and what some of the things that it could be made into.

He'd not written any self-help books before, and that had been why he'd been excited about the baby needs book. Actually, his was more like an awareness of things that were going on. But now, the entire book, a murder mystery, was completely written in his mind and he needed only to put it to paper. Putting his hands on the keyboard, he started writing. Christ, he had never felt this good about a book he was writing in a very long time.

He finally realized that he was hungry and leaned back in his office chair. He was stiff and thirsty, but he didn't have anything to drink near him. When he looked across the desk, he found Katie curled up in the chair and sleeping. That was also when he realized that it was dark out. Looking at the time on his computer, he was surprised to see that he'd been sitting here writing for nearly nine hours.

Picking up Katie, he took her to the stairs and carried her up to the master bedroom where she'd been staying since getting out of the hospital. Lying her on the bed, he was surprised again when she told him to sleep with her. Stripping down to his boxers, he got into the bed with her, and she wrapped herself around him.

When he woke up, the room was bright, with light coming from the windows, and Katie was still sleeping. Rolling her over so that he could get up to use the bathroom, she asked him where he was going.

"Bathroom. You need anything?" She said no and rolled over, and went back to sleep. He hurried through doing his business and climbed back into bed with her. "I love you, Katie."

"And I love you. I need you, Harman. Badly. Do you want me? Or do I need to give myself relief again while in the shower?" He lifted his head up and looked at her. "It's not really as satisfying as I thought it would be."

"Christ, I want you too. I've been, you're right, it isn't nearly as satisfactory as having you. You're hot, and I can smell you, your arousal. I need to taste you, now, I need to taste all of you. Thank you so much for giving me something that—I'm going to enjoy this so much, love."

He began to move down her body, licking and nipping at her as he went. By the time he had settled himself between her legs, she was wild with a need of her own. He could feel it, smell it from her. Being able to enjoy her because he was able to smell and taste her was the greatest gift that anyone had ever given him before.

When she leaned up on her elbows and he sat on his feet. His cock was hard and sticking straight out from his groin. Letting her look at him, stare at him, he felt his cock stretch even more, painfully more.

As she watched him, Harman wrapped his hand around his shaft and pumped his hand up and down. A drop of cum seeped from the tip. He watched as she licked her lips. It was perhaps the most erotic thing he'd ever seen a woman do. And she was all his. Watching her carefully, he told her what he wanted. But she said that she wanted him in her mouth.

"Christ, that sounds so wonderful. But no. Not yet. I would like nothing better than to have you wrap your mouth around me, but I want to taste you more. If you touch me, I swear to you that I'm going to come all over you, and that will be the end of our playing around." Harman promised her once again that she could have his body to do with whatever she wanted.

Blowing his breath over her curls, he was startled by the gush of cream that came from her body. Watching her clit swell had him wanting to pull it into his mouth to get whatever she was giving him. Harman needed to taste her as if it would cure him from certain death.

"Oh, sweetheart, you're wet, so wet I can see the dampness on your curls." He let go of his cock and touched her pussy. As much as he wanted to roll his eyes in the back of his head, he needed to watch everything about her, see her at her best.

His finger moved slowly along her nether lips by their own accord. Up and down like he had his cock to keep from leaping at her and taking her right then. Her body responded, and he saw her pussy weep more. He hadn't touched her yet, not touched her where she needed, where she begged him to touch her. When his finger slowly entered her heat, she opened her legs wider and raised her hips up to meet him. It was as if she was dancing—no, riding his fingers like she had begged him to ride her.

"Please, Harman. I want you. I—there's a need, something—I don't—I'm begging you to take me. You have to fill me, for me, please, fill me so that I don't die right here and now." Her hips moved up and down with his finger, and when he inserted another into her, she nearly came up off the bed. Whimper now, she moved faster with his fingers.

"I need to make you ready for me, love. You're too tight to take me inside of you yet. That's what you want, me to fill you with my cock, isn't it?" He was moving faster now; his body was on fire. He wanted to see her face when she came and it wasn't coming fast enough as far as he was concerned.

"Yes, oh yes, please." He felt rather than saw her move, her body straining to get to completion. While he needed to fill her with his cock, he needed to watch her when she came was even more desperate for him. When he felt her breaths coming in short gasps, she started to close her legs, but he held them open with his hands. She was panting now, her need making him ache to have her release.

With his fingers, he opened her lips and ran his tongue inside her, lapping at her, tasting her. When his mouth closed over her clit and suckled into his mouth, she screamed out her climax, but he didn't stop. While his fingers fucked her, his mouth teased and nipped at her until she came again and again. It was more than he could have hoped for in making love with his mate for the first time. More than that, he was sure anyone could have hoped for.

"Please, Harman, please. I want you. I want to suck your cock. Now. I want you to come in my mouth." As she reached for him, pulling away from his tongue, Katie pushed him back against the footboard. Helping her as much as he could without hurting either one of them, Katie leaned forward and stroked the length of him with just the tips of her fingers. His hiss made her seem bolder as she played with him.

"Take me, love. Take me in your mouth. I want to fuck your hot mouth and shoot cum deep into your throat." He was nearly sick with the need for her to take him. When she leaned over him, kissing the tip of his cock, Harman's eyes did roll to the back of his head, and he nearly fainted.

~*~

Katie swiped her tongue across the tip of the large deep purple head, taking the cream from his cock into her mouth. He hissed again. Bolder than she had ever been in her life, she wrapped her lips around him and licked again.

She loved the way he responded. He pumped into her. She didn't know what she was doing, but taking her cues from him and his body, she licked and nipped every inch of him, up one side of him, then down the other. When she felt his hand touch the back of her head, she knew that he was guiding her, showing her what he needed. Soon he was pumping into her hard, his cock bumping the back of her throat again and again.

"I'm going to come Katie. Fuck, I'm coming!"

Seconds later, she felt the first hot explosion hitting the back of her throat. He pumped harder into her, pulsing into her over and over. She swallowed him, his cum. Loving the salty taste that she knew was unique to him. He lifted her up and turned her over onto her hands and knees. She was ready, she thought, so ready for his cock to be deep inside of her. Moaning, she moved back against him.

Tensing up, she closed her eyes. Realizing that something was different, that he'd left her at some point, she turned and looked at Harman. He talking to her, telling her that she couldn't tense up. As he reached up beneath her, he cupped her breast in his hand and fondled her nipple softly while teasing her pussy with his cock.

"I can't believe how much I love you right now." She asked him what he meant, and he smiled at her. "I know that it's corny, but I think that I've been waiting for you my entire life. And now that you're here, I'm going to tell you just how much you have given me hope and love daily."

"Oh, Harman, I love you so much. Please. Will you make love to me?" Harman rolled her to her back and looked down at her. She knew what she looked like but didn't see anything in his face that said he was sick and tired of her. Or that he didn't want to make love to her.

Sliding up her body, he kissed her naval, her breast. Counting out each of her ribs, he nipped at them as well. It was slightly painful, the bites, but almost as soon as he ran his tongue over the little wounds, the pain was gone, and a feeling of being loved and cherished immediately followed. She didn't know that a person could cause pain in one breath and then claim that they're in love the next.

Harman played with her shoulder and bit into her earlobe. When he moved around her chin, he made a path that led him to her throat on her other side. The pain was a bit more intense as he'd bitten her just under her ear. However, she knew that he'd never allow anything to harm her so long as she was in his arms. Katie thought there was no other place she wanted to be but where she was right now.

Harman slid his body up hers. Taking her mouth in an almost savage way, she turned his hunger with a bit of her own. She wanted him right now, and when she felt his cock at her entrance, it was all she could do not to beg him to take her.

"Open for me, love." She did just that, wiggling her legs apart and then putting one leg on the other side of him. His eyes were closed when she looked up at him, and it made her smile. As soon as his cock was deep inside of her, her whole body moaned. Accepting him into her was like having her life complete. That, like him, she'd been waiting for Harman since she'd taken her first breath.

His warm hand slid down her body to her ass. Cupping it in his hand, Katie felt the connection to him better. As he moved inside of her, slowly, like he had found a place that he loved and he was moving in. As her body warmed up to his, letting herself stretch and hold him, Katie came hard. Just—she couldn't believe how easily she came and wanted so much more.

Wrapping her legs around his hips, she was happy when she figured out that she could lock her ankles around him tightly. Looking down to see where their bodies connected, Katie felt her mouth water, her pussy heating up when she could see his cock sliding into a very intimate part of her. It had her coming again, a short release that she knew was nothing compared to when they both came together.

With her hands held above her head while he made love to her, all she had to show him was with her hips that she needed more. Riding him, it was difficult to maintain a slow rhythm when he decided to go faster inside of her. Pulling her hand free, she reached up and dug her fingers into his hair and yanked as hard as she could.

"Fuck me." His eyes were glazed over, his face tight. She had to tell him to take her three times before it got through to him. "Yes, that's it. Fuck me, Harman."

The bed moved across the room. The pictures on the walls, mostly on the side they were pushing the bed to, shook and banged in rhyme with his strokes. Suddenly, he stiffened, and before she could figure out what was going on, Harman threw back his head and howled.

The climax took her. Her body stiffened like Harman's had, but it also felt like she was being turned inside out, over again. Grabbing for something to hold onto before she flew apart in micro pieces, her hands wrapped around Harman's biceps and screamed again. Christ, she thought, this was the most powerful death she thought had ever been experienced.

Harman dropped atop her, and she didn't mind. After a few minutes of his hot breath making her nipple pucker and move, he rolled to his back, taking her with him. Glad that one of them had the strength because she certainly didn't, Harman covered the two of them up and kissed her on the mouth before pulling her into his arms.

"I love you and enjoyed that immensely. However, we can't do that again. I don't believe that either me or my wolf will survive. Now, be a good girl and go to sleep so that when we wake up, I'm going to show you some tricks of my own." While she didn't know what he meant, she nodded and said she loved him as well. "I love you with all that I am, Katie Griffin."

She loved the sound of that but was too tired to try and figure out what tricks he'd said she'd done. Tomorrow, she told herself. She'll figure it out tomorrow.

Katie was in the shower when she remembered that she had an appointment today. Being the attorney for the family was proving to be a lot more than she'd thought it would be. Not that she didn't enjoy it. She was. Being busy all the time didn't allow her to think about anything but the job. For which she was thankful for. When her office phone rang, she answered it without hesitation.

"Hello, Katie, my dear. I was wondering when I could set up a time to speak to you about a few matters. I promise that I'm not going to badger nor beg you to come back to work for me. You've made the right decision, and I couldn't be happier for you and your new husband. How is Harman anyway? Happy as a lark, I'm betting." She told Jimmy Barnhart, senior, that they were very happy. "I knew there was someone out there for you. And you couldn't have gotten a better one than Harman."

"Thank you, sir. What time would you like to meet up? I have my afternoon free if that's a good time for you today." She heard him flipping through his calendar, which was forever on his desk. "Like I said, I'll be at a meeting until eleven, but you know that can run over quickly. But I'm popping out to get lunch around twelve-thirty. How about we meet at the little corner restaurant then?"

"Perfect. I'll see you then. Also, bring something for you to write on. I have a few things that I'd like to get settled before we leave. Mostly it has to do with the estate that we have." She asked him if he had a personal attorney for that, as she was better at business law than personal. "Yes, he's fixed up things for us. Mostly the way that you've written out for me. All the list has been done, too. Thank you for that."

"My pleasure. I'll see you then." She put the phone in the cradle and decided that she loved having a landline. It certainly did make it easier for her to sit still while working. As she was getting ready for her first appointment, Edwin knocked on her door. He asked if she was busy. "No, not at all. I have an appointment later, but I'm all right now."

She also told him about the meeting with Jimmy Barnhart, senior. She'd not realized that the Barnharts were good friends of the Griffin family and was happy that Edwin was all right with her leaving the office to take the meeting.

"We hired you, love, we don't own you. You can come and go as you please. I hope you know that." She said that she did. He was quiet for a minute or two after she handed him a bottle of water when she got up to get herself one. "I know that Jimmy wants now. It might be better if I go with you. Nothing bad, but you're going to want to talk to me about it as well, so I'll go with you."

"What's it about?" Edwin told her, including that she was going to inherit the Barnhart estate. "I knew he was going to do that. Rain explained it to me the other day. She also told me that the older couple was going to die. You have no idea how much it pains me to tell them that I'll see them when they return."

"I would imagine that it would. I know it has me as well. They're going to sell you the firm and their name so that you can get established as an attorney.

I think from all aspects, it's the best thing that could happen to you. For us as well. It would be Griffin and Barnhart until such time as you feel it could just be your name." She asked him how much he'd sell it for. "That I can't see. The magic is picky at times. But we'll purchase it with company money no matter what it is. Also, I think that you should have a couple of people working for you. You will burn yourself out if you try and do everything on your own."

"I know that I would." Edwin laughed, and she joined him. When he stood to leave, she asked him again if he was going to do with her. And when he said yes, she couldn't have been happier. "He was going to talk to me about some of the personal matters that will be left for me when they get to their home. It breaks my heart to know that they'll never make it."

Edwin joined her when it was obvious that neither one of them could believe that they would be gone by this time tomorrow. Picking up her box of tissues, she handed the box to Edwin, and she took it back when he blew his nose. After that, he left her, telling her that he'd see her in a little while.

Her client showed up forty-five minutes late. Then he acted like he was doing her a great favor by showing up at all. Tossing a sheath of papers toward her, she didn't even bother trying to stop it as it slid right off the other side of her. She did stare at the man like she dared him to tell her to get it.

"It's not going to do you any good if you don't know what it is that I'm having you do." The sneer is what got her. "How about you pick that up like a good little girl and I won't have to make a few phone calls to your boss on how you're treating me."

"How about you get your slick ass out of my office before I call my boss? And you certainly don't want me to have to do that." She did reach out to Edwin and told him not to leave yet, as she may have a problem. He told her that he was on his way back now. "You can't just expect me to drop everything after being so late, now can you? I actually don't care what your answer is. I'm not going to represent you on any level."

"You have to take me. I was told that you're new to this area and taking on my case—winning it too would be enough to have people clamoring to have you working for them." Katie told the man that she didn't need his kind of business. "How do you know? I might be the richest man around and you're turning down a good opportunity by telling me to leave. I'm not leaving in the event that you were being serious."

"She was being serious, David. And as for you being rich, we both know that's a lie. You barely make your dues payment yearly, not to mention being behind on your mortgage payment. I thought the last time you came around my pack members, I told you that I'd kill you. What are you doing here today? Beside harassing my attorney." She laughed, not even trying her best to stifle it when the man started sputtering about he'd not known she was his family. "Yet, Griffin is on the front door along with her hours of operation. Then again in the lobby, on her door that you had to open to come in here. And her nameplate, which declares her as Katie Griffin. Get out of here before I tell your daughter how you're going to be out of a pack if you don't leave now."

He left so quickly that he'd forgotten to pick up his paperwork that was still on the floor. Edwin picked it up and laughed. After showing it to her, they both got a good laugh again at the other man's expense.

"He likes to show off. I have no idea why he came in here. His daughter is his attorney, and that's all she does to try to keep up with his shenanigans. And trust me when I tell you, that's a full-time job for her, keeping her dad out of jail."

Edwin stayed with her until her lunch appointment. He knew about as much as she did about working as an attorney as he'd been one a few decades ago. Telling her that he kept up with his license because he wanted to have a heads up on the laws while serving his last stint in the service.

The little restaurant was the perfect place to have a business meeting. The place was decorated with the local high school logo and there were jerseys hanging up everywhere. Some of them were framed, and the rest stuck to the wall with push pins to keep them in place.

Even the inside was painted black and gold in the school's colors. Katie had missed the football season this year but was looking forward to it come next fall. Her love of sports and football was something that she dearly missed while working so much.

After they ate, Jimmy looked reluctant to bring up business. He'd been having a wonderful time, too. His face glowed with happiness. Then, when he did get down to work, he had everything that he needed to do for her lined up, with paperwork to go with it. Since it was after lunch, the crowd had left, and the three of them had an uninterrupted lunch meeting.

"I know this is a lot to ask of you, you only being the Griffin attorney from now on but I don't want to have to start over with a stranger. If you could do this for us, Hannah and me, then I'll be greatly appreciative." Katie told the older man that it was her pleasure to do that for him as he'd always been so good to her. "I sometimes think that I made you do more than your abilities, but you shocked me time and time again by getting things squared away. After a while, I just stopped thinking that you'd not get something finished up. You're a brilliant attorney."

"Thank you, sir." He nodded and handed her the paperwork that he'd just pulled out of his briefcase. "You want to sell me your business name?"

Acting surprised was hard to play at. She was surprised that he was actually doing it, and Edwin hadn't been kidding around with her. They couldn't lie to each other, but she didn't know if joking was part of lying.

"Yes. I decided yesterday that I could no longer go into an office every day and pick up—or I should say clean up the mess that Jimmy left me. It was just temporary, we told him when we put him there, and he's exceeded our expectations in fucking it up beyond what I thought he'd have done by now." She asked him how much, telling him that all her money was tied up in bonds and such. "No, no. I'm thrilled that Edwin is here with you. I'd like to have his company purchase it so that there isn't any kind of gossip spread around concerning you. You know as well as I do that people will still think that you slept your way into my heart, and while flattered, it couldn't be further from the truth. Hannah and I were talking last week about how we wished you'd been our daughter. Or I suppose great-granddaughter." They laughed.

"I don't know what to say to you. If the price is reasonable, we might just have a deal. But you've not said how much." After handing an envelope to Edwin, he laughed, and Jimmy did too. Pulling out his hand, Edwin told Jimmy that they had a deal. Did he want cash or a check? "You don't want me to know the price?"

It stung a little, but Edwin simply handed her the envelope. Inside was a small scrap of paper, much like someone would take a phone call number on. When she saw the number, she had to pull it out to really look at it. Edwin just purchased the entire building, contents as well as the firm name for one dollar. It was a good deal, she thought and laughed when Edwin pulled out his checkbook and wrote a check for the amount requested.

Katie so badly wanted to warn Jimmy and Hannah not to go on their trip. It was difficult to know that they'd both die and she knew all about it. But she'd been warned, no less than a dozen times, that to avoid a certain death this time would mean that they would surely die under much harsher conditions than before. She didn't know how dying by a plane crash could be topped, but she kept her mouth closed.

After they all parted ways and she headed back to her office, Katie asked for an hour to catch up on paperwork, closed and locked her office door, and sobbed for the stupidity of having magic if you couldn't save someone with it.

Chapter 5

It had been a long time since Jimmy and his wife had taken any kind of vacation. Even longer since they'd gone out to dinner that hadn't been attached to some kind of business thing. Tonight, they were enjoying a fine dinner and a glass or two of wine. Then, tomorrow, their adventure started.

"Are you sure that I don't have to pack anything?" He told her just a change of clothing was all that she needed. "Oh, before I forget, Jimmy, that wonderful young woman that you hired to settle our estate called. She has already sold the houses in England. My goodness, I don't know why we didn't think of this sooner. And to think that all you had to do was make a phone call, and things are moving in the right direction for us."

"I know what you mean, love. I think that by

leaving all the money and estates, she'll know what to do with our savings. With the one million left for us to enjoy our lives in a good way." Hannah smiled at him, and he felt like he could take on the world. Laughing, he thought about that too as he tossed the suits he'd only just packed out of his suitcase. "No more suits either. I won't get rid of them all, but most of them."

They pulled up in front of the restaurant, and he handed out his wife after he was out. Jimmy couldn't believe that it had been nearly seventy years since they'd met. All the way back in grammar school.

Celebrating nothing was funny to him. But they'd always been tight with their money. Not to go out to dinner at a good place to save money, and they both banked all their extra money in the form of IRAs as well as investing in their rainy day account. As far as he was concerned, it had been pouring for some time now, and he was going to spend the rest of his life pampering his lovely wife.

After ordering a plate of raw fruit and vegetables as their appetizer, they sipped their wine and talked about small things. What would they do with the furniture in their main residence now that they were finished with it? That was when Jimmy told her about changing the locks on all their properties. Leaving

Katie to get him the best dollar and for her to inherit their estate.

"I know that's the best way to do it. I'm just concerned for her welfare. She's the most polite person I know, and you know that Jimmy will eat her alive if she's not on her guard at all times. Poor child. I'm also very happy that we're not going to be here when Jimmy finds out that we really weren't going to leave him anything." He told her what the attorney told him. "So you leave him something, a small amount, and he'll know that you didn't forget he was our son. Dirty little fucker."

Jimmy laughed. When he'd been pursuing his lovely wife all those years ago, he thought her to be delicate, too. She was far from it, as he found out when she went with him on a dinner engagement for the firm. One of the guests had made a pass at her — Hannah was more beautiful today than she was all the way back then — and he still laughed to this day when he thought about his friend laying on the ground out the doors to their first home. There was his Hannah, sitting atop the man with her hand holding him down while she continued her conversation with the guest she'd been talking to. Jimmy would say to this day that that was the reason that he made her happy. His wife didn't take foolishness all that well.

Their dinner was steaks. He didn't care all that much, but he would eat them when his wife did. He had no reason in his head that he could think of why he did that, but it was a habit he didn't want to break.

His cell phone went off twice, vibrating in his pocket. Ignoring it to spend time with his wife tonight, she said she was going to go to the ladies' room, and he should check what was happening. As much as he didn't want to spoil their good time, he did what she'd asked of him. The first one was from the jail. The next two were from Katie.

After listening to Jimmy go on and on about what he wanted him to bring him in for dinner, Jimmy did wonder at his son being seemingly out of proportion with his previous eating habits. He'd been wanting green beans and mashed potatoes with his every meal. Jimmy had not eaten them as a child. What had he done that had him wanting them now?

Then, he listened to Katie's first message. She started it off by telling him that she was sorry for interrupting his night with Hannah, but she wanted him to know that their main house had sold just now and that Katie thought it would be a time for a celebration with that, too. The second message wasn't as chipper as the first.

"Jimmy, I wanted to let you know that Jimmy is going to be brought to the courthouse for his prehearing. I wanted to tell you that now in the event that you might want to go or not. I wouldn't if I were you. It's just going to be the same thing as he'd been saying all along. That he wants you to give him the house that he grew up in. And also that you give him his money now."

Hannah joined him as he finished the voicemail. Asking Hannah if she'd changed her mind about going to see their son before they left. Tomorrow would be a good way for him to be told that they were not going to support him any longer.

"I've not changed my mind. If you would like to go, I will be right there at your side, however long it takes." He laid his hand over hers. "I can't believe I'm saying this about my own child, but he's going to have to regroup and figure out how to make his own way in life. I'm finished with his ass." Jimmy laughed.

"You're a delight, love. An absolute delight that never ceases to amaze me. No, I've not changed my mind, but I did want to make sure that you hadn't changed your mind when I tell Katie that. She's sold our home, too." Hannah told him that was a cause for celebration. "Katie said the same thing on the voicemail she left me. I do need to let her know so that she doesn't need to reserve any seats for us. She said she thought the courthouse was going to be packed to see Jimmy get his comeuppance."

"Again, this is something else that I wished we'd done before." Shaking her head, Hannah smiled at him. "I know that we don't have much longer to be around. I'm well aware, too, that most elderly people our age have been shoved away in the nursing home. Jimmy, I never dreamed that you and I would spend sixty-five years together. I love you more today than I did then." He told her ditto, something that they'd been saying to each other since they met and had fallen in love. Then he told her how much he loved her.

After calling Katie and letting her know that neither of them had changed their mind, she wished them a good night, and he told her that they'd see her when they returned. If they returned. He thought that he'd like living on an island for the rest of his days. He and Hannah had a good night, just talking about the things that people their age talked about.

They talked about their age and how well they got around. He also knew that because his wife had done volunteer work at the nursing home years back, they were the exception rather than the norm when it came to their longevity. Both were in their early eighties and not sick or having too much wrong with them was something that very few people could enjoy without being in a great deal of pain all the time. Yes, sir, Jimmy thought. He was finally enjoying this time when the two of them were together.

It was much too cold for them to walk around the town after dinner. They got into their car, telling the driver to go where there were lots of Christmas lights they could see. For the next hour or so, that's just what they did. Enjoying the beauty surrounding them as well as the companionship of one another.

Going to the hotel, they had decided that they were too excited to wait for tomorrow's flight at home and wanted to get there on time tomorrow afternoon. They were going to pick them up a few things to tide them over so that when they got there, they wouldn't be smelling like well-worn travelers.

The hardest decision he had to make while shopping was the brown hat or the green. After considering it a few minutes more, he got them both. Still laughing, he found his wife looking at bathing suits. It had been so long since either of them had new clothing that it occurred to him that he had no idea what sort of things were in style anymore. For all he knew about fashion, he could have fit it in one of his new hats. Hannah showed him the one-piece bathing suit? Costume? He didn't even know what they were called anymore, and that made him laugh again.

"I've also brought us a few snacks for the plane trip. I know that they'll serve us dinner, but I'd like to start this new life on a fun note. Jimmy, I'm about to bust, I'm so excited. And being with you only? Well, I can't make you understand how that is exciting for me as well." He told her that he was, too, and laughed again. "I don't know that I've heard you laugh as much as you have lately. It's wonderful to hear that sound coming from you again, I tell you."

"You've no idea how lifting it is for me to laugh like this. I feel free. More so than I have in a long time. And I don't want to get us thinking about Jimmy, but I'm so glad that he's in jail while we're doing this. He'd find some way to screw this up for us." Hannah nodded and leaned her head on his chest while he continued. "I love him, honey, but I don't think I've liked him in a very long time. If we're being honest with each other, I feel too like a burden has been lifted from my shoulders in not having to deal with his crap anymore."

"I feel the same way. I don't care if anyone thinks

that I'm cruel, either. If they knew half the stuff that he's been up to since he'd been a child, they would actually feel sorry for us." Jimmy told her to buy both the bathing suits — she corrected him on what they were called nowadays. "All right. I think I will, and for good measure, I'm going to get the matching robe to go with it. In case I just want to run into town for a moment."

They purchased their luggage, just a couple of carry-ons to put their new things in. He wondered what people would say when they inspected their luggage and found that everything they had packed still had price tags on it. After the two of them had a nice cup of tea, Hannah said she was too tired, and Jimmy joined her in the big bed.

He couldn't sleep and slid out of the bed. With his wife still sleeping, he made his way to the computer to look once more at the house that Katie had found for them to buy. It would be just one more thing she'd have to take care of when they were gone, but this was something that he thought Hannah would enjoy as well. A lovely beach house with the ocean as their front lawn.

By the time Hannah was up and around, he'd found some things they could do while they were on layover. Not too much, they'd established that they weren't young anymore last night, and he found them things that they'd be able to see without too much walking around. When his cell phone rang, he took it, knowing that whatever news Katie had would be welcome.

"All right, the deed to your new home will be couriered to your new place the day after tomorrow. The keys have been given to the cook you now have. Ms. Lanton has passed her background check and is ready to start her employment with you two soon." He asked if he could put her on speakerphone, and she said that was fine. Repeating everything that she'd said to him, Jimmy laughed at the expression on Hannah's face.

"We've been saying this a lot today and yesterday, but we should have done this earlier in life. However, when I think on that, you wouldn't have been born yet when we were looking at retirement. Thank you so much, Katie. I hope you know how much we both love you." Jimmy could almost taste Katie's embarrassment but let it go. After that, Katie changed the subject and they were both fine with that. "The hearing is today. I'll be heading over there in short order. Oh. I nearly forgot again. The couple that are moving into your house soon wants to know if any of the furniture will stay. They believe that you've had a decorator come in, and they were that good."

"You've been in the house several times over the years. Is there anything in the house that you'd like to have?" He glanced at his wife, and she shook her head. "I've spoken to Hannah, and we want nothing from the house but our personal things. The rest of it can— They will be paying more for the house, and they're aware of that, correct?"

"Yes, sir, they are aware. I'll need for you to approve on the contents sales. I thought, after making a quick rundown on the household goods, I'm thinking that everything in the house should be about three hundred thousand. You've both been collectors for years, and it shows throughout the house. And since you've asked me. I would love to have your desk. Actually, your entire office suite. I don't have a set up at home just yet, and I would love to be able to sit at yours after all that you've done for me." Jimmy started to cry a little, and Hannah said that she'd be back. It was the kindness of this woman that made them feel better all the time. "I'll pay you whatever you think it's worth."

"You take it. Don't tell the couple buying the

house that you're getting it. They might feel like you're overstepping your bounds. But Hannah and I would be so proud to have you honor us by using my old desk."

After making arrangements to have the desk picked up, Katie said that she'd call him back with what the Connors wanted to do. After ringing off, he asked Hannah if she was all right.

"Yes. I so wish we could have had a daughter like her. I'm sure that she'd tell us that we were better off without her as a snot-nosed kid and that she's not nearly as perfect as we think she is. But I think that she is absolutely wonderfully perfect." Jimmy agreed with her. They were leaving the hotel soon to head to the airport and was glad that they had picked up some luggage to put a few things in. It made them not stick out like a banged-up thumb walking through the airport without even a purse for Hannah.

Getting on the plane, the two of them being sat in front of the plane in first class, had been a great idea, he told Hannah. They had room to stretch out as well as headroom that didn't have them bumping into the underside of the compartments that held luggage. Once he was finished stuffing their almost empty bags overhead, they settled down for the long trip across the country.

Jimmy must have dozed off at one point. He'd not gotten any sleep the night before, so he thought that a good nap would do him good. Hannah was doing a crossword puzzle, and he leaned back his head to relax while talking to her. Just then, the plane seemed to hit something, and he asked Hannah if she knew what was going on.

"I think that's what woke you up. It's turbulence, they keep telling us. Nothing to worry about." She raised her eyes from the book she was working in and looked at him. He could see the fear in her eyes and the way her face just seemed to be tense. "Jimmy, honey, I don't think we're going to make it to our destination. I have a feeling that all our planning to enjoy some time together is going to be these final moments that we're having right now."

Just as she said that, the plane nose-dived for a few long, tense moments before he felt it rise back up to cruising level. Instead of laughing off what Hannah had said to him, he reached for her hand and told her that he loved her. The lights flickered on and off several times before she told him that she loved him as well. They were both going to die, but they were together, so he was all right with that.

"We had a good life, didn't we, Jimmy?" He

assured her that there wasn't anyone that could say differently. "Thank you. For all you did for me over the years. I'm excited to be able to spend all of eternity with you again."

The plane dropped, this time starting a downward position that told him that they were going to crash nose-first into the water below them. A jarring stop after a few minutes had him sitting closer to Hannah. The seat belt light came on and the oxygen masks fell in front of them and the other passengers. Screaming started then. Everyone behind them was coming to the same conclusion that he and Hannah had already known. They were all going to die.

Items began to make their way through the air toward them. A pair of shoes hit him in the face. There were two books that landed on the wall between them. The next item, he thought it was a reader of some sort, it Hannah in the forehead, rendering her unconscious. He was happy for that. The less she would suffer, the better.

Holding her tightly again, Jimmy hoped for something to hit him as well. The waiting to die was long, it felt like. More items began to hit them as the plane made a slight adjustment, and now it was completely nose down, and he was straining then to even hold himself in his seat.

The plane just dropped quickly. While not too quickly in his mind, he knew it was fast approaching the ocean. He knew after a few seconds that they weren't going to come out of this one. Pulling Hannah so close to him that it tightened the seatbelt too snugly against his belly. But he didn't care. His only hope now was that they died quickly, that they'd not have to suffer overly much while doing so.

There was a brief hope that the plane might come out of it, but it was just his heart hoping. The reality of it was that they were too far from cruising altitude to recover. The impact on the water hurt him so much that he cried out once. Jimmy told his wife that he loved her again before something hit him in the back of the head.

Chapter 6

Carrie picked up the phone at home and said her name. She didn't know who would be calling her at this ungodly hour, but almost as soon as she was going to yell at the person for waking her up, she heard Katie sobbing.

"They're gone. Dead. Their plane went down over the ocean a few hours ago, and everyone on board was killed from the impact." Her first thought was that it was someone in Harman's family, and then she asked her who had died. "The Barnhart couple that I was telling you about the other day. They were going to live on a nice island and live out their lives happily. Now, I have to wait to find out if they find their bodies so that I can make the arrangements for their funeral. I'm so heartbroken, Carrie, I just don't know what to do."

"Did they leave you in charge of their estate?" Katie said that they had and asked her what that had to do with this. "Plenty. I want you to pull out your files and begin working on what they wanted. Has anyone told that man? The one that beat you to snot?"

"I suppose that would be left up to me as well." Carrie could hear the strengthening in her voice the longer they spoke to each other. Carrie continued to ask her questions about the estate, and she could tell that her cousin was getting stronger all the time. "I know a little about the estate. Rain told me that I was to inherit everything so that I would distribute their wealth to the right places. She also told me that they were going to crash and not survive, but she didn't give me any details. I'm thankful that they were together when they breathed their last breaths. I've never met a more dedicated couple to each other than the two of them were."

"That is what I think about when I would see you and Harman together. Devotion as well as undying love. That's the two of you, too." She thanked her cousin. "All right, let me tell you my news. Joey and I are moving to the States. Can you tell that I've been practicing my proper English?"

"I did notice that, aye." Carrie thanked her.

"What are you going to do when you get here? I'm assuming that you're going to live close to us. Please, please, please?"

"We are. There is something else that I need to make you aware of. Joey found out just as we were getting home. I'm not supposed to tell you this, but Belinda has cancer. She has it in her blood, and they don't know if there is any hope for her. Joey is devastated, as you can well imagine. The kids don't know, but I think they know that something is going on. My heart hurts for them all the time now."

"Oh, those poor babies. And Joey. She's not that old, is she? I mean, older than us but not by much." Carrie told her what she knew. "Thirty-five. I'm so heartbroken for that as well. I know that they have small children, and I loved meeting them. I hate that... there is so much that Belinda is going to go through with this. I wish I could do something for them all."

Carrie and her cousin talked for another hour. She not only made Katie feel better, but she did as well. After hanging up the phone, she got up. There would be no—

"Holy fuck. Where did you come from?" The woman said she'd come to help her family. "My family? What do you...who are you?"

"Storm Griffin. I missed meeting you when you were in the States. But duty calls. Your cousin, Katie, is my sister-in-law. But I came here because I didn't know where your brother lives. If you could give me an address, the two of us will pop right in there and out again, and no one will be the wiser." She asked her what they were going to do. "Make it so your sister-in-law doesn't die. I'm sure that no one wants that. By the way, you're fixed up too. No more cancer on you, either. It was very kind of you not to want to tell your cousin, but I believe Katie is much stronger than you guys give her credit for. What's your brother's address?"

Carrie didn't know what was going on, but she prattled off the address where her brother lived. Knowing it by heart, she could have driven there blindfolded. After being told she could open her eyes, Carrie hadn't even realized that she'd closed them. The two of them were standing in Belinda's kitchen. The very person they had come to see was sitting at her kitchen table sobbing into a napkin. Not caring what her friend and sister was crying about, she pulled her up from the table and hugged her tightly.

She noticed the look on Belinda's face when Storm hugged her. It was like she was in pain and shock at the same time. After getting another hug from Belinda, they sat down with her at the table. She started talking about how the cancer hadn't been caught soon enough, so there was little they could do for her other than to make her comfortable at the end.

"You have nothing to worry about." Belinda thanked Storm and told her that it was going to devastate her parents when they found out. "Then don't tell them anything. But I think you misunderstood me, Belinda. You really have nothing to worry about. The cancer is gone, and you're as healthy as…I was going to say ox, but that's kind of rude. I'm trying to work on my tact at telling people things. How's it working so far?"

"I have no idea. I don't know anything about you, but for what little Joey knew about you and your husband. Are you really the queen of all wolves?" She said that she was and smiled. "That is so awesome. I know a few wolf shifters around here. They really keep things on the low down so that people don't know…I guess humans don't know. I think people would be upset about finding out about them. But to…you said that the cancer is gone? How is that possible?"

"I'm very magical. I've made you immortal. Your entire family is now. Including the child that you carry." Belinda put her hand on her belly and looked at her husband's cousin. "She didn't know either. As I said, I'm very magical. So is my sister, Rain. We have this thing going about how to outdo the others when it comes to this family. We love the Griffins so much and consider you a part of our family as well."

But I've only just met you. What if I'm a terrible person?" Without answering her, Storm just smiled. "As I said, I don't know you, so that could be a good smile or not. Tell me what you're saying to me so that we're on the same page."

"You're an immortal. You won't ever die. Not if you're shot in the heart or have your head removed. That last one is something that you should avoid at all cost. You'll still be alive thanks to my magic, but you'll also be headless. Best let that one never be a problem." Carrie wasn't sure if she was joking or not. As Belinda had been saying, they didn't know the woman. "Also, because you're now a part of this family, you have wealth beyond anything that you've ever thought of. And since I know you were all planning to go to the States, thinking that Joey would want to move on, you'll have a lovely house, staff, as well as a job. Though you never have to work, there will be a job too that you can step into as soon as you're ready."

"This is too much." Storm put her hand on

Belinda's. "I just don't know what to think about this. I mean, I've only been…will my children stay little like they are now? I don't know, wouldn't that it would be such a burden to have them at this age all the time, but I'm sure that people will talk."

"They'll grow up and age until they're twenty-five or so, then they'll simply stop ageing. Believe it or not, Harman is thousands of years old. So is his entire family. Also, and I find this is the best perk of all. You'll never gain weight unless you're breeding, what they call a woman with child, then that weight will simply fall off in a few days. Your children will be safe too from any kind of diseases as well as long term hurts. They can be hurt, don't get me wrong on that, but there will never be a life-threatening thing for you to worry about. To any of you for the rest of your long lives."

Carrie looked at Belinda and then at Storm. Her head was just wrapping things up about the information, but it really was too much to be thrown at someone who was new to the magic. She finally found a question that she could ask without making herself look foolish.

"You said that we'd have wealth. Break that down for me in terms my brain can handle. When I spoke to Katie while there, she was worried about the money that she had and wondered if it would be enough to carry out her dreams." Storm asked her what the dreams were. "Oh, well, she wanted us all to be together from now on. I think that one is about to happen. But she wanted an old building where she could have her practice and where she could see people crossing the street if she were to look out. I think she had that or something like that at Barnhart, but I've never been to their offices."

"Mr. Barnhart sold her his name, his public name, so that she could attach herself to his clients. After a few months, he wanted her to drop his name and just use hers. Edwin was also able to purchase the building that they had offices at. It will be Griffin Law Firm when all is said and done. Katie will be taking on cases for the family, but she'll also do other work that is near and dear to her own heart." Carrie asked if it had been expensive. "A buck. So no, not expensive at all. Jimmy told Katie and my mate that he was just too old to go back to working as an attorney to straighten out the mess that Jimmy had made. In order for her to prosper, he did it this way so that Jimmy would also be out of a job."

"That's wonderful for her. I do hope she takes the biggest office and has windows put in if there aren't any there now. I bet…well, she'll need a few weeks to get over the death of the Barnhart's. The way that Katie spoke about them, I think they were closer than boss to employee." Storm told her what she'd heard. "Yes, I can see that, especially after meeting Jimmy. Having her for a daughter would have been a perfect blend for Katie. However, I can't help but think that she'd not be what she is today if she'd been pampered — just an idea on how they would have treated her."

"You're more than likely correct on that." Storm looked around the room, and Carrie did as well. The place that she was living in wasn't all that much different than the house where they were currently living. A dump. Belinda had done a wonderful job of making it less dump-like and more homey. But a dump is what it was. She looked at Storm when she said her name softly.

Belinda had gone to answer the phone, so it was just the two of them at the table. Telling her that this was all any of them could afford, she knew that there was a bit of a bite to voice. Storm didn't laugh at her. Nor did she make any kind of comment on living conditions.

"We're not a wealthy family here. No one is, actually. I think that's why Joey is so keen about getting out of here so that his kids will have a better chance than we've had. My parents are both gone and so is Katie's. But Belinda has family, and they are very…unpleasant to be around. I think it's been several years since she's had contact with them." Storm told her that they didn't like that their child was living in such conditions and blamed it squarely on Joey's head. He'd have a better job had the two of them not blackballed them all over town."

"Ya see. I knew that they'd done that." Belinda sat back down and asked what she'd missed. Storm told her, and she could see on Belinda's face that it had been Joey on the line. Then she told her the sad news. "He's been fired? For what reason may I ask?"

"He missed too much work." Belinda started crying and held her daughter on her lap, who was trying to comfort her mother. After a few minutes, Belinda looked at her and smiled. "I'm finished with the lot of them. My sister told Joey when he was fired that she took great pleasure in having him being terminated. And she'd continue to do so until I got some sense in my head and came home. Only I can't bring the children with me. They want nothing to do with them as they're, and I quote, 'damaged from having a sorry drunk like their father.' Joey doesn't drink. I've never seen him with even a beer in his hands in all these years."

With Storm's help, they were able to get things squared away with the houses. Carrie didn't even want to go back home to get some of her things. But in the end, since they were leaving here first thing in the morning, Carrie was going to have to sleep there one more night. Also, which she thought was hilarious, they weren't going to mention anything to their landlord or Belinda's family. Not even later, Belinda told her.

Carrie made her way home after having dinner with the Griffins. Katie had been popped in, as well as Harman, to celebrate, and she was shocked once again by the look of love they both had on their faces. She wanted a love like that someday and hoped that it would come along soon. But she was immortal now. Perhaps she had a little while longer to hunt down her mate. Laughing, she pulled a shirt that was miles too big for her over her head after undressing and got into bed.

Tomorrow was going to be a good day and spent with family. She could hear Joey laughing in the other part of the house and wondered if Belinda had told him about the baby and no carcer news. Rolling to her side, she looked out the broken window over her bed and watched the cars fly by. Since the houses were so close side by side as well as front to back, there had never been a yard that anyone could play in. She wanted that, too. A magical place to raise her children. Yawning, she closed her eyes to get some rest. Tomorrow was going to be exhausting, and she couldn't wait.

~*~

Katie didn't offer her condolences to Jimmy. It had always been a strained relationship between him and his parents. And now that they were gone, she'd come here today to tell him, he just sat there with his wrists in cuffs. There was a large eyebolt in the middle of the table. The officer told Jimmy that if he started acting up, he'd be locked down or back to his cell in no time.

"So they're both dead. At the same time." She said that since they'd been sitting in first class, that was where most of the damage had happened. He looked at her and laughed. "They wouldn't eat fish or anything close to that, and now they're fish food. Kind of ironic, don't you think?"

With a pop to the back of Jimmy's head, he was chained to the table. She felt like she'd been given some kind of hope when he'd first agreed to speak to her. Now she knew there was no changing for some people. Especially him. Taking out her notes on things that she'd been asked to go over with him, she crossed off the top two. He'd been told about his parents and also been told there wouldn't be a burial for obvious reasons. She looked up at him.

"You're named in the will. Don't bother asking me what it has in it. I don't know. The reading of it will commence on Friday early morning here at the jail so that you can hear about it when everyone else does." He asked if he was getting everything. Then he said that he'd better be getting everything. "As I told you, I didn't write it out for them, so I have no idea what it says. I do know that I've been asked to liquidate their real estate as well as any stocks and bonds as needed to keep their charities working. I don't know how much law you remember, Jimmy, but—"

"I'm a damned lawyer, Katie. And you'll address me as Mr. Barnhart from now on. I'm going to go through everything that Dad left up to you, so don't get too comfy. I'll have you out on the streets again in no time." He was handed a thick pad of paper so that he could take notes on things that he needed to go over with his own attorney. "We'll just see how all my land is sold off when I'm in charge. I should be right now, but I'm biding my time right now to see how fucked up you make things for me. How much is their estate anyway? They worked like they were going to be around forever and never spent so much as a dime of all their money on me."

"I do believe that they bailed you out every time you got into trouble, Jimmy. If I remember correctly, that was about weekly. Not to mention, you've been knocking around people who had to be paid off because of the lives ruined. I don't know what's in the will, but I know that if I was in charge of writing it out for them, I would have told them to leave you access to a buck. Because of you, they were never asked to go to garden parties, which your mother loved, nor the club. They'd asked that you not be brought there again several years ago."

"Like I care. The place was boring, and I wasn't allowed to touch the staff anymore, so that got boring fast, too. I tried to liven the place up, but all they did was turn me away. They'll be begging me back now. I'll have Dad's money, and it'll be a showdown for everyone that looked at me in that side-eyed way." She told him that he didn't know what he was talking about. And asked him why they'd welcome him back because his dad was wealthy. "Because I'm going to have all the money, duh. The first few weeks after I get out of here, I'm going to stay there all week, never leaving until they understand that this Barnhart cannot be told what to do."

"Whatever floats your boat, Jimmy." He told her once again to call him Mr. Barnhart. "No. Now, as for the next reason that I'm here. Each and every creditor here and abroad has been warned about you being able to charge anything, steal, or think that the Barnharts were going to be there for you. You've broken that bridge down all the way to the river." He said that would change now that he had the money. "Again, you go on dreaming about that supposed money."

Katie didn't let him bother her. She wanted to go home and cry some more, but that wouldn't bring them back. It hurt her in ways that she'd never had before to know that they'd not be around for her first child and her happiness now that she'd found her one true love in Harman.

"What else do you have for me to listen to you going on about? Is there any way that I can get this finished so that I can go back to my cell? Lunch will be served soon, and I have put in a special order because my parents have kicked the bucket."

He grinned at her. She knew that he was trying to get a rise out of her. Ignoring him while she packed up her things, he was asked to sign off on the list of things that she'd told him. And, of course, he had to make a big production about that as well.

When she was in the main lobby of the station house, she was so happy to see that Harman was there waiting for her. He'd told her this morning that he'd try to make it, and even though she told him it would be all right, she was thrilled to see him. And to have him hold her.

"Mom and Dad invited us to have dinner with them. Dad said that he could understand if you wanted to skip out. It hurt them both to know that you'd lost such a good friend in the Barnharts." She said she'd rather not go out. "I know that they'll understand. We'll eat in. Maybe order some Thai food or something.

"That sounds wonderful." She waited for him to place an order for them and then turned and leaned on his chest. It was awkward for being in a car, but he was warm, and she felt like she was living with a cold heart for what had happened in the last twenty-four hours. "You don't think that they changed their minds about the building, do you? If they left Jimmy in charge, I know that it would be a living hell for me."

"It's doubtful that anyone in my family, including my parents, would allow him to be around much after being released. I'm not saying that he's going to be killed by them, but he won't be around to bother you anymore." She looked up at him. "I'm not making any promises that it won't be Story nor Rain either, but as I said, he'll be gone. Could be the entire family wants to get their two cents in on his death."

"You're serious." He nodded, then winked at her. But she still worried that... "You know what, I don't care who does it. It'll be wonderful to have him out of our lives once and for all time."

They made their way to their fast becoming their favorite restaurant, too. Harman went in to get the food but came back out empty-handed. She was so disappointed that she had to fight tears over that. She just wanted one thing to go right, and it should have been the food. Now she was going to have to go home and —

"They want to give you a hug." She just stared at him. "They said they heard about the Barnharts and knew that you were close to them. So they want to show their respects and hug you too."

She got out of the car and slowly made her way around it. The icy roads were terrible, so she was careful not to fall and break something important. Laughing when Harman picked her up so she'd not fall, she was giggling when they entered the restaurant.

The two of them ended up staying in to eat. Mostly, it was because their car had been snowed in when the plow trucks came down the street. Harman said that he could dig it out but wasn't worried about it. When she looked at him, his head back and his eyes closed, she knew that he was enjoying his newfound sense with smelling.

"It's a small wonder that I didn't eat here all the time. Had I been able to smell things, I would have been in trouble for just hanging out at the door until they opened again." She knew what he was talking about, but hers was with being in love with him. He made everything spicy and hot, calm and wonderfully still. She told him how much she loved him, and he kissed her on her mouth. "Let's get to eating this before I come to regret not taking you home with me to be able to make love to you all night."

They made love all the time. It didn't matter what room they were in. He'd press her against something sturdy and take her that way. Or he'd put her up on a dresser or counter and eat her until she was exhausted with it. Even the dining room wasn't off-limits to them. Anywhere and everywhere, the mood struck them. They were tearing at their clothing and going at it.

The desk had been broken in the day that it had

been delivered. It had been exciting, too, because the delivery people hadn't left the house when he'd tossed her onto the big desk and fucked her hard. Christ, just thinking of Harman and his cock made her feel all hot and sweaty.

Today and late last night, she'd been going through the things that had been left in it. Things that she knew that he was humbled by, not to mention, there were personal notes from Hannah that he'd kept in his top drawer. Love letters that had been written as late as the day that they'd left the house to go to the hotel.

She'd not realized that it was stuffed full of items that Jimmy had left in it. There was an entire drawer in one of the cabinets that was filled with accolades that he'd received over the last few years. She was sure there were more someplace in the house that he'd kept for sentimental reasons. Letters from families, too, thanking him for helping them when they needed it.

She put them in a box, thinking to give it to Jimmy, but she decided that he'd just toss it out. It would mean a great deal more to her than him any day of the week. Leaving them in the drawer, she decided to go through them when their passing wasn't so fresh. Getting up when someone rang the doorbell, she looked before opening the door.

"May I help you?" She spoke to the person on the other side of her locked door as she had no idea who the man was standing there was. "I asked you if I could help you."

"Yes, you can start by opening this god damned door. I'm not going to be conducting business with you this way." She told the man that she wasn't going to discuss even the time of day with him until he told her what it was he wanted. "I just told you. I need to conduct some business with you. Unless you're some worthless housemaid or something. Open. The. Door. I'm not fucking around with you."

"He can't come in if he means you harm." She looked around when Storm spoke to her. *"I'm at home, but that man, he can't enter your home with any intention of harming you. Just open the door, and you'll see. He can't come in."*

"All right, but if he hurts me, I'm going to blame it all on your ass." Storm laughed. *"You'll have to tell me sometime how you knew that I was afraid. I'm assuming it has something to do with your wolfy magic."*

"Wolfy magic? I love that. Yes, it had everything to do with that. Just open the door, and you'll see. Also, you'll need to remember this, you're an immortal." That wasn't all that reassuring, and she told her that.

When she laughed, Katie opened the door. That was when she noticed that there were several large wolves just behind the man. That helped more than Storm's words of wisdom.

"About damned time." He couldn't enter. No matter how many times he tried, and he did try a lot, he couldn't get past the barrier that was there. When he pulled out a gun, pulling the trigger all in one movement, the bullet freakily stopped at the door jam and dropped to the ground.

The man, whoever he was, didn't have time to marvel at the things that had happened. He'd disappeared. Just gone. Stepping out onto the porch, she looked at the trail of blood that ended at the outer edges of the decking. Looking at the wolves that were lying down now, she asked the one in front if she was supposed to know them.

"*I should hope so.*" It was Edwin who introduced each of the wolves to her. All Harman's brothers and their father. Sitting down on the porch steps, he had to put her head between her legs and breathe slowly. "*Honey, are you all right?*"

"Since you didn't tell me which one is Harman, I'm going to assume that he's off doing wolfy business with that man. I don't want details, but a simple nod would be fine." Edwin nodded. "And this wolfy business that…I have no idea why I'm asking this, but I'm assuming that he won't be bothering anyone ever again."

"That would be a good assumption. Yes." She wanted to smack Edwin on the blunt of his nose but didn't know if she could get up quickly enough to bar him from the house and attacking her. At his laughter, she glared at him. *"You're kind of cute when you're upset. Did Harman tell you that?"*

"He knows better than to screw around with me when I'm upset. Do you know anything about that man? I mean, there is nothing we can ask him now that he's wolfy food." She gagged a little. "He won't eat him, will he? I kissed him…tell me that you don't eat the people that you take care of."

"We don't." She let out a sigh of relief that she was sure people at the next town over could have heard. *"We do, however, tear them to bits too small for anyone to see. There will be blood, I suppose, but that's easily explain away, too. There will be a missing person's report, I guess, but –"*

"Shut up. Just close your…what is that called that is full of teeth." He told her it was a mouth. "On a wolf, you dumb ass. I know what it's called in human language, but…never mind. I'm going into the house now. You can come or go. It's entirely up to you."

She sort of wanted him to come in. Not wanting to think about the man, she decided that she didn't want to be alone. As the million questions kept circling the drain to her mouth, she wanted to shoot questions at Edwin until she understood more of what was going on.

When he entered the dining room, she'd been using it as a makeshift office, she continued packing up the things all over the desk. She only had to glance at him for a moment before she saw that he was clothed now that he'd shifted to his human side.

"As you're aware, I'm going to be taking over the estate for Mr. Barnhart. I'm going to use some of his money to open a law office that is free of charge to anyone who needs legal advice. They won't be taking on cases, not at the office, but they can do what they wish after hours. Violations of that stipulation will mean their licenses will be revoked. It's a nice loophole that I've used before when it came to copyright infringement." He asked her if she was going to have lawyers ready to take the cases. "No. I'll have the people take a list of professionals that deal with whatever their problems are and they can pick from there. I'm not allowing any cases to go out from that office because I don't want a conflict of interest to get in the way."

"That sounds kind of tricky to me. But then, I've not been an attorney for some time now. All right. We'll support you on this. I'm assuming too that you won't allow attorneys to lay out pamphlets or anything to sway the people coming in." She told him that she wouldn't and would keep an eye on that for issues. "Good. It sounds like you have it under control then."

"Except for one thing. I need a building. I don't want the foundation involved because I'm sure that people will find some fault with that. Instead, I'd like for you to lend me the money to buy the building. It will have to be a sale because, again, people will talk." He said again that it was tricky as well. "You've no idea. There will be law books there as well. For attorneys that can't afford their own that they can use or borrow, I guess. The books can be taken home. I like that idea, but if they don't return them, then they'll be charged the full amount for the book as well as banned from using the place again. I don't want to fill out someone's law library by having people steal what is there."

Harman joined them in her new office just as she was carrying the boxes she'd packed into the room. The books, all law books, were on the shelves, too, and she couldn't have been more proud than she was seeing them all lined up the way that Jimmy had had them.

Twice now, she'd had to pinch herself when she had a moment of thinking things weren't real. Even her love for Harman would catch her off guard, and she had to sit down for a moment and breathe because she was so nervous. She called herself lucky. In all her life now. However, it didn't make her any less afraid that the other shoe was going to drop and soon.

Chapter 7

Tony only just noticed the boy who was down between two cars. He was watching the traffic and waiting. For a moment, he thought that the kid was going to jump out and in front of the car that was speeding down the street.

It was warmer now, but it didn't make the clothes that the kid had on any less appropriate. He was wearing a white tee shirt that had seen better days. Not that it was too dirty, but it was worn in places that showed more skin than it did in keeping the kid covered. When he looked as if he was going to jump again, it was all he could do not to reach out and grab him by his too-large jeans.

"Nah, you don't want to use that car." The boy nearly fell into the traffic and only just barely got back to his place. When he turned and glared, Tony just grinned. "You're going to need a newer car. That way, you can be sure that they'll going to be able to replace the car when you're killed. No, it's better to use a new one."

"What do you know? I might have a ball in the street or something." Tony didn't bother pointing out that he didn't even have any shoes on, but the kid seemed to get it. "Things are tough. All over."

He'd heard that from some adult, he'd bet when telling him that they couldn't afford anything much anymore. Tony had seen that time and time again around here. Things really were tough. But killing himself wasn't going to solve anything, he told the kid.

"You have no idea." He turned his back on him and watched the cars. "That was a good idea that you had about cars. I wouldn't want my parents to have to pay for a new car, too, after I'm gone."

"The next car is Mrs. Weddle. She's like ninety-three. If you jump out in front of her, you could kill her, too. She's one more heart attack away from pushing up daisies as it is now." The kid nodded. And stayed where he was. "What makes you think that being dead is better than being alive? Things will turn around. I don't know when, but they will."

Without turning, the kid answered him. "My dad

has been out of work for almost three years. My mom lost her job at the diner when they closed up last week. Something about not having the right foods anymore. I think my mom cooks the best food in the world but some people just don't care for comfort food anymore." He told him that he'd not known that the diner had closed down. "The post office is trying to get that place closed down too. She told her boss that it was stupid for her to be paid by mailing out one envelope a week. At least she's getting paid."

"That is true." He told him about the next three cars. One of them being his wife. "She'd beat your butt if you didn't get killed. Then she'd hug the stuffing out of you. If I were you, I'd not let any of my family hit you. It wouldn't end well for you."

Although he thought that it might end very well for the boy. His family would take them in, and they'd never have another worry. But he needed to talk to this boy to figure out why he thought that jumping under a car would solve his worst problems.

"My dad, I heard him telling my mom that he was better off dead for them. That got me to thinking that there was just one too many people to feed. And if it was me, instead of my dad, then things would be all right for them. I had to think on this powerful hard,

Mr. Griffin. I have me a little sister at home now, and I do love her." Tony congratulated him on the birth of his sister. "Thanks. She's a tiny little thing. Cries sometimes late in the night, but she's all right. I love to feed her the bottle. For such a little thing, she can empty one faster than I can count to a hundred."

The boy, his name was Cody Banks, he knew now wasn't watching cars. Tony wasn't going to take the chance that he'd changed his mind, so he kept a good eye on him. When his mom came and sat with him, he told her through their link what was going on. She promised him that she'd not say anything to Cody.

"Did you come around this morning and get those apples that I wanted you to take to the pig farm, Tony? If you were busy this morning, you should have told me. I would have found someone else. They probably could have used the ten dollars more than you anyway." Cody stood up and moved over to where the two of them were. "Well, hello, young man. I didn't see you there."

"Mrs. Griffin, I can take care of those apples for you. Mr. Arbon said that pigs will eat anything, including people." Mom told Cody that she'd be happy for him to take them as Tony was too busy watching the streets. "How many bags do you have? I bet you made some delicious jelly with them. Mom says you make the best apple jelly from them worn-out apples of anyone she knows."

"Thank you, Cody. That was very sweet of your mom. While you're at the house, make sure that you pick up a couple of jars of it. There some — oh, I have so many things scattering around in my brain that I have to get done. Would you mind working for me? I don't just mean today, but, well, all my workers are married now with kids, and it will fall on me to get the house looking good." He told his mom she was making him seem like a lazy ass. She laughed and told him that this was a good cause. That he should make his way to the Bank's home and figure something out there. Mom was still talking to Cody, guiding him away from the streets to her home. He'd have a pocket full of money before the end of the day and more than likely fixings for dinner. Tony loved his family so much.

The next family member that sat next to him was his baby brother Stone. He looked worn out. Asking him if he was all right got Stone looking up and down the street like he was being chased or something.

"Women are coming out of the woodwork after me. One of them actually told me that this is their last chance of snagging a wealthy husband in me, and they'll all clamoring to get a piece of me. Like I'm the prized cow or something." Tony laughed, and Stone told him that it wasn't funny. "Everywhere I go, there are a herd of them. Waiting with food in their hands. I know how to cook, damn it."

"It's part of that old saying. You know it. The way to a man's heart is through his stomach. That's what they're hoping for, that you'll pick them because of how well they cook." Stone told him that was stupid. "Yet here it is going on. When do you start school back up? I know that you've been on Spring break. Won't be too much longer will it? You'll be safe in the school. Right?"

"You'd think that. But no. They come there with the pretense of talking about their kid's grade. Ms. Marbel doesn't have kids, not only not in my class but even in school anymore. I tell you, it's like I have a target on my back when I go out." Tony laughed, and the two of them started down the street. "School is going to be out another week. We have too many school days left over, and they're wanting to use them. I don't know why that would be an issue, but the board said that we can't teach too many days or we'll get in trouble. I miss my four walls."

"I need some help. Not really help so much as I

need advice. Harman asked me to look at a building that he's thinking of buying. He needs one for writing space. According to him, there is too much going on at home for him to write. I think that it's because he's forever chasing his wife around the house and forgetting about working. I do the same thing. That's why I no longer work from home. Too distracting." They both laughed, and Stone said he was actually looking forward to that someday. "She's out there. I swear it. And when she comes around, you're going to be knocked for a loop, and that will be the end of you being chased around by strange women."

The little house that he was thinking about for his brother would have been perfect for an elderly couple or one just starting out. It had two bedrooms, which was one of his requirements, and a kitchen. The other rooms, while they would be good for the space, he didn't really need them. As they walked around the room, Tony enjoyed the views from the windows, wondering if that would be a distraction, too. It would be for him.

"There's even cable running in here. I believe that its central heating and cooling is gas too. That'll be nice. I love gas heat. Gets my toes warm faster." Tony rolled his eyes at his brother as he went from furnace grate to grate, testing the heat coming from it. "I'm seeing if the heat is disturbed well. Like the ones over the furnace, will they be hotter while the rest of the house is cooler? You have to know these things."

"Yeah, sure. I'm sure that Harman is worried about getting too hot. As if any of us worry about that." Stone said that was a good point. "Moron. I have to admit that I do love this tiny kitchen. He can have a nice lunch made without having to travel home or out. Sometimes, I forget to eat when I'm working on a large project. Also and this might be me remembering wrong, but doesn't he have like a million books? They'd be nice all shelved up in the living room. Take up the carpet and put in wall-to-wall bookcases. In there, he'd even have someplace to sit and read them if he wanted."

Even though he'd not called his brother to okay the house, Tony decided that if Harman didn't like it, then they'd find someone else who could live in it. Visiting relatives would enjoy having a nice little place if they were visiting their families with a bunch of young ones. Getting away might be the difference of getting invited back next year.

Just as they were leaving, him having called the realtor to pull it off as a listed place, Harman joined them. And his shirt was on inside out. Stone got to point it out to him before he could, but he loved the embarrassed look on his brother's face.

Harman walked around the little house with them then. Both he and Stone pointed out the things that they'd thought of around. When he said that it would be perfect, Tony thought that his brother would be about moved in before the ink dried on the deed.

Going to three more buildings that he'd been looking at, his brothers Edwin and Garfield joined them. Jeffery, who had been working with something hush-hush, joined them at about the time they were making dinner plans. Tony knew that his wife was taking the kids to their favorite place tonight, and he would have had to eat alone. This was so much better.

"Why don't we call Dad. See if he wants to have dinner with his boys. I'm sure he's not too busy to do that." Edwin said that he'd call him and make sure that he came with them. Tony called the local restaurant and made the reservations for the seven of them. Tony told him that Harman was with Dad and that he was coming in. He couldn't remember the last time that Dad and his brothers had dinner together. This would be epic.

They were just being seated when Dad brought

up the Banks boy. He was telling them that Mom had pushed him out of the house right in the middle of a project to have the boy do it.

"It wasn't as if I didn't want to do it. I was already nearly finished. Then she picked up my screwdriver that I was using to put the last screw in and took about half of them out. Women are a little bit of a screw loose, too, if you were to ask me." Tony laughed and told him what was going on. "He was going to kill himself? Well, that's a different can of worms altogether. The kid can only be about ten or twelve." Stone said that he was fourteen, and that got them all to thinking.

"I have an idea that when he overheard his father saying that he was worth more to them dead, he was thinking insurance. I'm betting right now that none of them have insurance now that they're out of work, too. I'll have my wife look into that for them." Tony thanked his brother for that. "No problem. I want to help, too."

The rest of the evening was spent talking about the changes around the town since it started growing up around them. The biggest change was the buildings. Of course, that would be it. Trees, too, that they planted along the main drag were so big that the county was thinking that one or two of them needed to be taken down, they were that old.

"Remember that old trading man? The one that would come around with his wares once or twice a month? I was in the cemetery the other day, Mr. Harper's momma died, and I was there for that, but I found his headstone. Got me to thinking about all the things that are different." Edwin asked if he'd been the man who had been kicked in the head by his horse. "It was my mule that kicked him, but yes, that's him. He couldn't be told what to do without some kind of backtalk. So when he went ahead and stepped into the street behind my mule, he was dead before he landed across the street. The reason that I bring that up is one of his daughters, Lilian June had herself seven daughters, remember them?" Every one of them groaned when Dad asked.

"There was never a group of women born that wasn't as homely as they were. Nor were that all that nice if I remember correctly. One of them was as big as me. Nearly seven feet tall. And hands? Good lord, they could pick up a grown man by reaching out and grabbing his head without any trouble. Why did you ask Dad?"

"I was contacted by one of her great-granddaughters the other day. She and her family want to come into town and have a memorial for the man who started it all. Old Taterhead Blue was his name. She asked me if I ever knew his first name, and it took me until today to remember it. Sebastian. Sebastian Blue. But he was called Taterhead for nearly all his life, I think. It's even on his headstone out there." They talked about more people that had gone through their lives after that. Trying, Tony thought, to outdo the one that had the best memory.

"Dad, tell the story about how Harman got his first name. I think that will top all the other stories." Harman looked at him and asked what he was talking about. "You were named after one of the biggest characters ever born. Just let Dad tell it. It's a good story.

"Well, now, let me think on it a bit. I want to get the story set like it was back then. Boy, oh boy, that was a deep memory for me. Hadn't thought of it in a long time. All right. I have it now. It was just before you were born, Harman."

~*~

Charlie could see it all in his mind's eye. The street hadn't had a good rain in a long time, so it was spitting up dust every time something blew over it. Just a mess, he told his sons, a right mess all the time.

"We'd get these little spurts of rain that would make it worse. Then, the dirty rain would stick to everything a person owned. Even the horses were sick of being dirty and dusty all the time. Then came along Wayne Harman. I think that was his name, wasn't it, Edwin?" He said that it was. "Had him a wife, too, but she didn't stay long. To this day, we don't know if she left town on her own or if Wayne sent her home. But she was just gone one day." Charlie had always thought, to himself, that he'd killed off his wife by accident one day, and that had been the end of her. "His clothing wasn't cleaned up anymore. That was the first clue. But she was just a tiny little thing. About five foot nothing and about as big around as my leg. I swear to you, I never seen a couple more opposite of each other than those two. Him a big honking man, and her this stick wife woman. Anyway."

Charlie still had bad dreams about what had happened that morning. He told his sons, not at all ashamed that he'd shed a few tears when Wayne had met his death. But before getting to that, he told them about how he'd become a character.

"He'd paint his face. Whatever suited him that day, he'd be all painted up and come into town on his little bitty horse. I swear I heard that poor pony sigh every time he would get on him and off. But he always had a carrot or two for it, and I guess it didn't mind so much." Dad laughed. "The day before he passed on, he'd come into town as a clown. Now, I want you to imagine about the ugliest clown you've ever seen just coming into town with his face all painted up white and a big nose. Didn't have a tooth in his head either. That sort of put some people off, but not the kiddies. They just loved him." Edwin spoke then.

"He always had a bag of some kind of treat, too. Sometimes, it would be a bit of rock candy that he'd made or a book with a couple of pages in it. It was terrible, just a few words, but Harman had made it him himself, and that was fun, too. One time, he had cotton candy. A treat that I'd never tasted before then." Charlie nodded, his memories of the things coming to him faster now. "I'm sorry, Dad. I didn't mean to interrupt your story."

"You didn't. You helped me remember some things. He made the cotton candy machine, too. And the way he would have it made over those hot flames would entertain us for days after he left us." Dad laughed then. "Never did he come into town empty-handed either. Even if it was just a few coins, pennies mostly that he'd hand out to the kids."

Smiling, he continued. He knew that it was a sad smile. He felt his hurt for the man all the way to his toes. Nodding, he continued talking about the man. A man that had become his friend the day he'd been killed.

"One day, he comes riding into town and has himself a string of ponies behind him. About twenty or so, all of them walking behind him like he was piped Piper. They were attached to each other. Nope, they were just following him into town like he was their leader. He found me coming out of the store and asked me if I needed some ponies. He told me that they would need to be around us a lot so they'd get used to our smell." Tony asked his dad if the town had known that they were wolves. "No. And I, to this day, don't know how he figured it out. Just asked me right out if I wanted any. So shocked was I that I nodded my head before I could think on it too long."

Charlie shifted on his seat whenever he thought about the next part. "He was a good man. Upstanding. I thought for a long time that he might well have killed his wife off. I still have thoughts like that, but not as often as I did back then. But Wayne, he was walking away from me, and he told the ponies, the first one, that they belonged to me from now on. And wouldn't you know it? They stayed right there with me like I was their new master or something."

"What happened, Dad?" He looked at the man's namesake and had to dust away a few tears then. "Dad, you don't have to finish it if it's going to upset you. We can move on."

"No, no. I want to tell you." Charlie cleared his throat before beginning again. "I had Edwin start to take the horses to the barn. But he was stopped by a group of men who thought they should have the ponies more than I did. I really would have given them to them had they only asked, but they didn't. Jumping on them and trying to get them to go home with them. Nary a one of them moved but looked at me, frightened and all."

A pony died that day. The man that had been seated on him had beat him to death because he wouldn't move. Another one had to be put down. He, too, had been beaten up so badly that there wasn't any coming back from it. He didn't tell the boys that. It hurt him to know the cruelty of some people.

"Wayne, hearing the ruckus, came back to see what was going on. One of the men in the crowd asked Wayne how he'd come to have such fine ponies. And then he asked him if he was some kind of wizard or something. He didn't know what that was and looked

to me for help. So I told them that they'd have to explain
what they were talking about as Wayne didn't know.
The man who had asked didn't wait for an answer but
picked up the closest thing to him and bashed Wayne
over the head with a piece of firewood. Well, now, I
told you he was a big man. Had a thick head, too, and
all that log did was splinter in a few places and didn't
seem to faze the big man. He was polite, even though
there was a bit of blood going down his face that the
man not hit him anymore. It hurt his head. Then he
looked at me."

Charlie blew his nose hard. The tears were
coming faster now, and he just didn't care. He'd told
his sons all their lives that it was all right to show
emotions when they got the better of you. And that's
what was happening right now. His memories and
thoughts were getting the better of him. Putting his
handkerchief away, he began telling of that day again.

"Wayne picked up Edwin and Tony, set them
right on those barebacked ponies, and sent them to the
house. That's all he said to them, to the house. Once
they were out of the way, the boys, not the ponies, all
the men there turned on Wayne. I got myself beside
him and pulled out my gun."

"You have to remember that not many people

had guns back then. Nary a rifle, either. They made do with what they had, and a gun purchase would have cost them more money than they could use to eat on for the year. So I pointed my gun at the group of angry men and told them to back off. Then I made sure that they knew that I'd be working with them on the sale of the ponies if they still wanted one." Charlie looked beyond his sons and saw the street that day that it happened. "Mr. Hartman, he was the meanest man alive. I thought he said that he wanted Wayne to go and get him some fresh horses. I wasn't sure what he meant by that, but it wasn't the answer that he wanted. It was more than anyone had that day. Like I said, he was a mean person."

"You gave the ponies to Mr. Griffin. Why didn't you hand them over to me? I have me a nice ranch out there, and I would have given you top dollar for them. A man run down like you are, I'm betting that you could use some cash in your pocket about now." Wayne told him that he really didn't need the money that the earth provided him with everything that he needed. "Oh, so you're rich, are you. Tell me how much money you got on you, and I'll double it if you take me to get them ponies I'm wanting."

"I don't have any use for money, not much to

speak of really, but the land and the earth, they provide me with all the things that I need. Apple trees. There was a peach tree out there, too, but I missed them growing. I put me a few vegetables in the ground early spring, and that's been — "

"I don't give a good damn about your gardening. I want you to show me how you got them ponies, and then you're going to go out with me and get me some more." Wayne had tried to explain that he'd not had anything to do with them coming to him. Most animals liked him. "So I'm guessing that a hare or something will bounce his way up on your table all cooked and everything when you're hungry."

"Now you're just being silly." The anger that had come over his face still scared him to this day. "How would it know how to cook himself?"

The knife came out of nowhere. It was still dangling from Wayne's chest when he reached out for Mr. Hartman's horse and took it to the ground. When it was obvious that Mr. Hartman was going to shoot him this time, Wayne reached down and snapped, just like it was no more than a bit of sticks, off his arm and threw it away.

"The townspeople just went mad after that. They ganged up on Wayne and beat him to death. Even after he was dead, they still kept up at it until it was difficult to tell that the mess on the street was a man." Charlie looked at Harman. "The clouds came out of nowhere and were just bursting with water; they filled the streets with water. As we all stayed there, still in shock at what had happened. The body of Wayne Harman was fading into the ground. Like he'd was being a part of the earth that he had loved all his life."

"What was he?" Harman asked Charlie again what the man had been. "Was he a faerie or something? For the earth to have taken him back, he had to be something special to someone."

"He was special to everyone he helped. And he did help a lot of people when he could." Charlie thought of something else while thinking about the man. "You're named after a great man, Harman, and if he were here now, he'd be proud to know that you've carried on his works with all that you do."

Charlie wanted to change the subject and was thinking that he wanted to let his sons know how incredibly proud he was of them. But before he could get the words out, the six of them said that they loved him very much and that they were proud to have him as not just their father but a great role model, too. His heart was full at that moment, and he was sure that he'd think about this night for the rest of his days. He still shed a tear or two of happiness that he'd been a part of raising such wonderful children.

Getting home a great deal later than he meant to, Charlie sat on the deck and watched the trees. Closing his eyes when a small spark appeared, he waited for the mother earth to join him. He wasn't the least bit surprised to see her then.

"You've been telling the story of Wayne again, haven't you, my dear friend? I bet you left out, as you usually do, that you were hurt too when the mob came after him." He said that it wasn't part of the story in talking about how Harman had gotten his name. "Perhaps not, but it showed me, once again, that a better man couldn't have been chosen to help the earth. Thank you for that."

"'Tis my pleasure, my lady. Forever." When she sat down, there was tea and cookies for the two of them. "I shouldn't indulge. I have a big day tomorrow and I'll be too full to enjoy the breakfast meeting that I'm attending."

He sipped his tea first and then took a couple of cookies. Charlie knew that they'd be his favorite and wasn't disappointed when he bit down on the first one. As they enjoyed their tea and cookies, not a word was said about anything so earth-shattering but the warm weather that they were enjoying.

After she told him of the things that she had in her life, he told her that they'd help her in any way that they could. Grace told him that she'd take him up on that and get back with him. Charlie made his way to his wife and bed just as the sun was cresting over the trees. He didn't need much sleep but knew that he was going to be extremely tired for the rest of the long day. But he couldn't have been a happier man than he was when Luna wrapped her warmer body around his and kissed him. Charlie thought again how lucky he really was.

Chapter 8

Harman walked down the hall toward the room he had been requested to go to. Ms. Donahue had asked if he could come to see her, and he told her that it would be his pleasure. As he was backing out of the room, finding her sleeping in her bed, she turned and looked at him with a huge smile.

"I'm having a better day today. Come, come in. I would like to talk to you a spell." He came into the room and sat down in the room's only chair to do what she requested. "My granddaughters have been in to see me. I remember them sometimes only as they're leaving. It hurts my soul when I remember bits and pieces of the things that I said to them. Will you tell them I'm very sorry?"

"I can do that. Is that what you wanted to see me about? I don't mind coming to see you, Ms. Donahue.

If you need me, have one of the nursing staff call me at home." She nodded, but Harman wasn't sure what he was supposed to be doing. "Can I make things better for you in here? Anything you want so long as it's approved by the staff to —"

"You used to call me a pain in your backside. But you were forever kind to me. Still, to this day, I can't tell you how many times I thought of you. You become a bigger saint than the one that I had in my heart all those years ago." He laughed with her. "I remember the day of the dance like it was yesterday. You saved me so much in the way of humility that even my family doesn't know about."

Harman put his hand over her very frail one. Kissing the back of it, he knew that he couldn't save her, but he did give her a little bit of himself so that she'd be better the next time Carrie and Katie came to see her.

"All I did was be at the right place at the right time, that's all." She nodded, and he believed that she was doing what she said and making himself out to be a saintly man. "You were so beautiful back then. You still are, I think; however, aging has made you more so. And I've noticed too that you've not lost your ability to say what you mean either."

She laughed with him and closed her eyes. "It was like yesterday to me. There you were, all dressed up for the prom, and no one that was at your home to take you. I bet you still have the corsage, too, don't you?" She said that she'd pressed into her diary and that it was still there. "You gave me a wonderful time as well. Dancing around the floor while standing on my feet. Thankfully, no one had noticed.

"They would have been relentless to me had they known that the class bully didn't have the first clue about dancing with a handsome man. My goodness, you look just like I remembered you all those years ago." He told her it was clean living. "Yes, and I'm a monkey's uncle. But I still remember you growling low to that boy who asked if he could dance with me. You do know that he turned out to be my late husband? He was. And we had such wonderful years together after we married."

"I'm so happy that you found your one true love. I have, too, in one of your granddaughters, Katie." She said that Katie had told her. When she stretched out in her bed, he helped her fix her tangle of covers. "They give me one every time I tell them I'm cold, but don't take the old ones out. By the end of the day, my blanket collection weighs more than I do." It was then that she told him the reason that he'd been asked to come see her.

"I know that you're not human. I think I knew back then that you weren't. None of you Griffins are, I think." He told her what they were, and she smiled. "I was thinking bear, but that's near enough to something that gets all furry."

She closed her eyes, and he watched as her chest rose and fell to her breathing. It was getting slower all the time. Her heart was strong, too, but he'd bet his last nickel that she was going to pass on today or tomorrow. Looking at her, he could remember the beauty that he'd taken to prom the only time he'd ever gone in her face. The same violet eyes were not as lively, but there was a spark there. When Hope turned to look at him, this time, she had tears on her cheeks.

"I'm going to die. I had plans to live out the rest of my life in my home with my sister, but she didn't wait for me. Now I have to go it alone. Do you think she's looking down on me and wondering what is taking me so long?" Harman told her that not only did he believe in the afterlife, but he was looking forward to joining up with some of the friends he'd lost.

He didn't tell her that he couldn't die but didn't think that one small lie would get him into trouble.

Harman smiled when he remembered the things that he'd helped her with to get her popular.

"Was it at all what you thought it would be? Being the belle of the ball and so on? I've often thought when I'd see you around town with your crew that you didn't like it any more than I would have." She laughed, then coughed. It was about time, and he knew it. He decided to tell Hope some things about himself and his family, knowing that she'd not tell anyone else.

After telling her how his father had come to be pack leader, he told her how they'd been working and investing in not just business people but regular humans, too. She smiled again, and Hope closed her eyes again.

"Even though my parents could neither read all that well, in my mom's case, she couldn't read at all, but we were happy. And happy to be able to help some of the townspeople that needed it." Hope asked him if he'd helped her family in some way. "Yes. Not as often as many but we did make sure that you could reach your mortgage payment when it was coming due, and one of your sons wasn't working to help out."

"Those boys of mine were a lazy bunch. The only thing that they excelled in was getting on my last nerve. And eating everything that we had in the house.

You'd think that I was being selfish about letting them eat, but what they couldn't eat, they'd destroy what was left." She slipped away, her dementia making her act out for a few moments. When she demanded that he go away, he only touched her hand, and she settled again. He was wondering what had happened to her sons when she spoke again.

"David was all right. He still had his moments of loving us, his parents. But then he'd go with Roger, and that would be the end of that." She wanted to get this off her chest, and he was going to make sure that she was able to do it. "I killed Roger one night. Just walked up behind him with a gun and blew his brains out before he was able to kill his father."

"Do you want me to see to his body? I don't mind doing that for you." She shook her head and told him that they'd never find either of them. She'd raised pigs on her little plot of land. "Good for you."

"I didn't know what you'd say to me about it. I thought…well, it goes to show you, Harman, that you don't know something, then ask. I'm so happy I could tell you that. His daughter doesn't know. Neither of them do. And if you'd tell them for me, after I'm gone, then I will sing your praise to anyone up there—If I go to heaven, I'll tell everyone what a good man and friend you turned out to be." He told her that she'd go. She had protected herself and her family. "If the good lord sees it that way, I'd be appreciating that."

Between naps she would wake and tell him something that her sons had done to her and her husband. It was terrible, he knew, to have one of your children treat you so badly that you were made to kill them off. He asked her about David.

"It was tricker to have him out of the house. When his brother disappeared, he accused us of killing him. He even came out and asked his dad if he'd killed him. Saying that he'd not had a thing to do with his death, then telling David that he might want to straighten up, still has me smiling. And you know what, for the next few years, he didn't come around all that often. He had Katie with him when he did. I guess he figured that we'd not kill him with his little girl was around.

"That was about the time that they all packed up their things and moved off to parts unknown. It wasn't until years later that we realized that they had gone to Wales. Moron, he didn't know the first thing about the country and came back here when he couldn't take it anymore."

"And Roger's wife, she stayed there too, I'm assuming. That's why the two of them, Katie nor Carrie, knew that much about each other. They're catching up now. The two of them are having a good time getting to know one another." Hope said that was the way it should have been. "But it's made them into the people they are."

"Hogwash. Everyone says that, but it's not true. Katie was lonely all her life. Kids wouldn't become her friends because of her being so smart. I think she was that smart because she didn't have anyone to play with when she'd been just a little thing. I do think that at some point in her living with us that she thought we'd killed her father. But she didn't come to us about it. She's a smart one, that little girl." Harman agreed with her. "But David, now there was a mean, cruel person. I akin him to being related to Genghis Khan. He was that mean of a man. Anyway, one night, I was sitting in my car, waiting for one of them car services to come and change out my tire for me. It was raining, oh lordy, was it ever raining that evening, or I might have noticed the car that pulled up in front of me."

He held her hand while she rested. The nurse came in to see if the monitors were on her right it wasn't registering very well. Instead of allowing her to wake her up, he convinced her that things were just fine.

"He got out of his car with a tire iron in his hands.

Waving it all around, he broke out my front window as well as the driver's side. He'd not hit me yet with it, but it wasn't for him not knowing where to swing it. Every which way that he could, David was hitting it. Then the fool hit me in the head with it thing." He could still see her lying on the road with her life's blood draining out and being made lighter because of the rain. "Your daddy, he was there, I remember. So was that...I think they were all there when the police made their presence known to me."

Harman decided to come clean with the rest of her story. "My dad killed your son. As soon as he came up on the scene, he shifted into his wolf and tore his throat out."

Hope turned her head and looked at him. He wasn't sure if she'd believe him or not, but it was the truth. She asked him how he'd known what was going on. Told her of the time she'd broken her ankle with being the mother so soon after Roger had been born and you begging him to fix you. That you'd never tell—"

"No, I hit him with the tire iron to keep him from hurting me anymore." He told her that Dad, his dad, had taken that memory away so that she'd not be ridiculed about seeing a man turning into a large wolf that saved her life." Harman could tell the moment that she remembered it the correct way. "He told me that he didn't want me to go to prison for killing a man that was going to be the death of me. So he fixed my ankle by giving me a bit of his magic. That's what really happened, isn't it?"

"Yes. Dad talks about you often. How you got a bit more of his magic than he'd first realized. He said that was why you healed up so quickly and never got a cold ever again that might harm you." Hope cried, and he let her.

One thing that he did know was that David didn't die that night, nor the next. His body, along with his brothers, were never found either. Being wolves, they could smell where the grave was of Roger and dug him up to put him into a safer place. One that didn't get trampled on all that much and maybe discovered.

"I thought that's why you are forever baking him things when you're able, and he eats the whole thing by himself. I know that he felt, and still does, that David was set to kill you, and there wasn't a thing anyone could do to stop him but a big black wolf full of anger." Hope told him that she'd been ready to die but so wondered about Katie. "Which was wonderful because she is my mate. The love of my life."

They sat there, the two of them, and talked. Hope would doze off, each one longer than the one before. Her heart had stopped beating a few times for a full minute. Every time, he was ready to call the medical personnel in to revive her. But she told him she didn't want to be revived. That she was ready to go see her husband.

Harman sat with her for another three hours. Assuring her that he was still there because she didn't want to die alone. He told her several times that he could call in her granddaughters, and she wouldn't have it.

"They'd be all emotional, and I wouldn't be able to handle that." He agreed with her but continued to ask her what she wanted. "You think that you can pay for me a nice jar to put me in when I'm cremated? Anything will do. Even if all you have is one of those butter cups that had a tight lid on it."

"I think that I can do better than that. Where would you like to be hanging out with us? Over the mantel? Maybe so close to the food that a little bit of you falls into our dinner?" She laughed, and it took its toll on her. "I know. I'll sprinkle you over the graves of your sons to prove to them that you outlasted the two of them."

"I'd like to be on your mantel if Katie doesn't mind." He assured her that she'd not mind at all. "Good, you just stuff me behind some picture up there and you won't hear another peep from me."

When she closed her eyes this time, he knew that she was gone. But she surprised him to no end when she woke up and looked at him again. "Will you dance with me, Harman? One last time?"

"It will be my pleasure, Hope." He put his hand on her shoulder and gave her images of the two of them dancing down the halls here. When she passed, her dream of dancing with him still in her mind, he got up and kissed her soft cheek, and sat down again. The staff, having been alerted by him that she was gone, came in and told him how much she'd been looking forward to talking to him. "When you called me, I dropped everything that I was working on to come here. I wouldn't have missed this for the world."

After telling Katie and Carrie that she was gone, he made his way to the police station. While he'd been talking to Hope, he told his dad that it was time for the earth to give up her dead. That Hope had asked him to do that for her.

"'Tis something that I've been thinking about when you told me where you headed. I've already moved their bodies out to the fields. And with a bit of magic from Rain and Storm, it looked like I'd been out there testing the dirt for the spring planting, and there they were. Both of them lying side by side."

"Thanks, Dad. You're the best there is." Dad told him that he was humbled today, and that all his boys had been by to wish him the best. "We should have a cookout. To celebrate life coming full circle."

And it had. Things had a way of working around things and he thought that this was a perfect example of it. Two men would be found, and a great lady was going to be laid to rest. He wondered what the next chapter of his life was going to bring. Harman was excited for it to come around.

Before You Go...

HELP AN AUTHOR

write a review

THANK YOU!

Share your voice and help guide other readers to these wonderful books. Even if it's only a line or two, your reviews help readers discover the author's books so they can continue creating stories that you'll love. Log in to your favorite retailer and leave a review. Thank you.

AWARD WINNING, BESTSELLING AUTHOR

Kathi Barton, a winner of the Pinnacle Book Achievement Award and a best-selling author on Amazon and All Romance books, lives in Nashport, Ohio, with her husband, Paul. When not creating new worlds and romance, Kathi and her husband enjoy camping and going to auctions. She can also be seen at county fairs with her husband, an artist and potter.

Her muse, a cross between Jimmy Stewart and Hugh Jackman, brings her stories to life for her readers in a way that has them coming back time and again for more. Her favorite genre is paranormal romance, with a great deal of spice. You can visit Kathi online and drop her an email if you'd like. She loves hearing from her fans. aaronskiss@gmail.com.

Follow Kathi on her blog: http://kathisbartonauthor.blogspot.com/

www.ingramcontent.com/pod-product-compliance
Lightning Source LLC
Chambersburg PA
CBHW032010170626
46807CB00006B/2742